W9-BGJ-373

THE MYSTERIOUS CARAVAN

WHEN the Hardy Boys take a winter vacation in Jamaica, Joe finds an ancient bronze death mask washed up near their beach house during a violent storm. Did it come from a Portuguese galleon wrecked offshore centuries ago? Why are three treasure hunters determined to snatch the relic at any risk? Is it because of the cryptic Arabic words concealed in the mask?

Helping the Hardys and their friends in this bizarre mystery is William, a Jamaican boy, who flies to New York with startling news, only to be intercepted and held for ransom—the death mask!

How Frank and Joe rescue William, plunge into their father's airline-ticket theft case, and fly into a maze of danger in Africa will hold Hardy Boys fans breathless to the last page of *The Mysterious Caravan.*

Frank and William raced for their lives!

Hardy Boys Mystery Stories

THE MYSTERIOUS CARAVAN

BY

FRANKLIN W. DIXON

NEW YORK
GROSSET & DUNLAP
Publishers

CONTENTS

CHAPTER I

The Face in the Sand

WIND shook the flimsy seaside cottage and banged a loose shutter with such violence that Joe Hardy gave a startled jump. "If this gets any worse," he said, "we'll be blown right off the island of Jamaica."

"And they advertised no storms at this time of year," his brother Frank said with a laugh.

The two boys, along with four high school friends, reclined on cots in the beach house they had rented for a ten-day winter vacation. A candle they had lit after the power failed gave a fluttering light for several seconds before expiring. Now they were talking in total darkness, trying to be heard above the crashing surf and screaming gale.

"Feel this place swaying?" Tony Prito asked.

"Like it's dancing the calypso," Biff Hooper added as he adjusted his big frame for more comfort.

1

"All we need now is a steel-drum section," was Phil Cohen's comment.

Bang! went the shutter again.

"Whoops!" chubby Chet Morton said. "Let's see if we can fasten that plagued thing."

"I wish we had a flashlight," Frank muttered. He felt his way to a front window and reached out for the slatted cover, when he noticed lights tossing on the cresting seas.

"Hey, fellows! Look here! Somebody's in trouble!"

The others jumped up to peer out into the maelstrom.

"Incredible," Phil said. "That boat won't stay afloat for long!"

"There she goes!" Chet exclaimed.

The lights disappeared for a few seconds, then shone feebly again.

"She slid down into a deep trough," Tony said. "How can she take such a pounding?"

Once again, amid the whistling gale, the lights disappeared and the boys waited anxiously. But it stayed dark.

"Probably capsized," Biff said.

"Come on, let's try to help," Frank suggested. "If a victim is washed ashore, we might be able to rescue him."

The others agreed and stepped out into the storm. They were all young and good athletes. Everyone except Phil was on the high school

football team. Phil was a lightweight, but fast as
a cat and he held the county tennis championship.

Eighteen-year-old Frank, and Joe, a year
younger, were the sons of world-famous sleuth
Fenton Hardy. But they had become detectives
in their own right. Starting with *The Tower
Treasure,* their careers spanned many adventur-
ous cases. The last one, known as *The Clue of
the Hissing Serpent,* had carried them to far-off
Hong Kong.

"We'll fan out along the shore," Frank said.
"But don't get pulled into the surf."

The velvet sky was streaked with low scudding
clouds, providing a ghostly backdrop for the palm
trees that were bent nearly double. Fronds and
branches skittered along the sand like giant spi-
ders seeking refuge from the storm.

In seconds their sneakers were soaked, and
they were drenched to the skin by rain. The
hissing surf chased them up the sand; then when
each gurgling wave receded, the boys ran to the
water's edge, peering through the gloom for possible survivors of the shipwreck. There seemed to
be none.

Separating farther from one another, the companions strung out, trying to cover as much of the
shore as possible. They knew the sea currents
could be tricky. People might be carried along
the beach for quite a distance.

Joe had raced on ahead of the others. He

searched the sand near a spit of land, where palm trees bent close to the water's edge. Did he see something? He moved forward cautiously toward an object lying at the foot of a palm tree and bent down to examine it.

"A timber!" he said half aloud. "A ship's timber. I wonder if——" He heard a crack, then nothingness.

The large branch that hit him on the head lay beside the supine boy as the tide continued to rise. The waves lapped over Joe, rocking him to and fro.

Meanwhile, the others had searched in vain for survivors and struggled back to the cottage. They entered, skinned off their wet clothing, and toweled down. Frank fumbled in his suitcase for a change of underwear.

"Hey, Joe, did you borrow any of my things?" he asked.

No answer.

"Listen Joe. I definitely remember I had another pair of shorts here. Joe? Where are you?"

"He isn't here," Chet said.

"Where is he?" Biff asked.

"Who knows?"

Frank felt a shiver of fear climb his backbone. Had Joe been sucked into the raging sea? Surely his shouts for help would have been drowned out!

"We'll have to find him!" Frank declared.

"Let's go!" He put his damp clothes on again and ran out into the gale. The others followed.

How long Joe had lain unconscious, he did not know. The last thing he remembered was the sound of the cracking tree. Now he heard the surf, felt it filling his ears, nose, and mouth with bitter saltiness.

The water was about to cover him completely. Joe moved, and a pain stabbed the back of his head. "I hope it isn't fractured," he thought. Wincing with every movement, he inched higher onto the sand. The effort exhausted him, finally, and he stopped a few feet above the collar of suds lacing the beach.

He flung out his arms and breathed deeply, praying for the air to renew his strength. His left hand felt the wet sand, but his right rested on something the size of a coconut shell. It felt slimy.

The boy's fingers studied the contours of the object and his pulse quickened. "Good grief!" he thought. "It feels like a face!"

Could this be a victim of the shipwreck, half buried in the sand? Thoroughly stimulated, Joe raised himself on his elbow. At the same time he heard shouts in the distance. It was Frank and his friends.

"Here I am, over here!" he rasped, the taste of salt burning his throat. He struggled to his knees and called out again. They heard him and rushed over. Eager hands pulled Joe to his feet.

"What happened?" Frank asked.

"I got conked by a palm tree." Joe gingerly felt the back of his head. He had a bump the size of a large egg.

"We'll help you back," Biff said, and he steadied the injured boy with a strong grip.

"Wait a minute," Joe said. "I think there's a body in the sand. You might be stepping on it."

"Where?" Tony asked.

"Right there."

Tony and Phil dropped to their knees and felt about.

"Argh! Here it is," Tony said. His hands found the face, slippery and covered with sea moss and barnacles.

"Careful as we dig," Phil cautioned. "If it's been in the water long, it might fall apart."

Biff still held onto Joe as the others clawed the sand from around the face.

"Hey, it's a skull!" Frank cried.

Phil felt it. "Half a skull," he said with a shudder. "The back of it is sheared right off!"

"Leave it be," Chet advised. "In a voodoo place like this I want nothing to do with a skull. Its ghost may come to claim it!"

"What are you scared of?" Frank asked. "This might be a help to the authorities. It could have been a missing person."

"It feels like a face!" Joe thought.

"Most likely a murder victim," Biff said.

Joe bent down impatiently and picked the thing up. It had not felt like a skeleton to him. He remembered the cold lips and firm chin. "We'll take it back to the cottage," he said, "and examine it there."

All five trudged along the beach, with eyes still peeled for possible bodies from the shipwreck, but had seen nothing by the time they entered the beach house and shut the door behind them.

Phil, who had a medical career in mind, got the first-aid kit and applied medication to Joe's bump.

Frank fixed the shutter while Biff lit the candle on the table. They all pulled up wooden chairs to look at Joe's find.

"See. It's not a skull," Joe said. He pressed his thumbs into what should have been soft flesh.

"Hard as a rock," Frank observed.

"Suppose it's ossified?" Tony asked.

"Hardly," Phil said. "Not in the water."

The light flickered over what appeared to be a man's face. The nose was straight, the chin firm with a curly beard.

"It's some kind of mask," Joe said. He pulled out his penknife, flipped open a blade, and was about to scratch away the covering of sea growth when Phil stopped him.

"Hold it," Phil said. "This should be done by an expert, or it'll be ruined!"

"What about you?" Frank said. "Didn't you work for the museum once?"

"Right. I restored old artifacts. That's why I was worried when Joe tackled it."

"Well, can you do it?"

"I'll try. But no guarantees!" Phil took the knife and started to work on the mask. "It's metal," he said after a while. "See it shine?"

"Am I glad," Chet said. "No skull, no ghost!"

"Where do you suppose it came from?" Tony asked.

"That's anybody's guess," Frank said.

The boys watched, fascinated, as Phil worked on the mask carefully.

"I'm glad you're feeling better about the ghost," Tony ribbed Chet. "I didn't know you believed in spooks."

Chet grinned wryly. "You never can——"

His words were cut off by three loud raps on the door. They all jumped!

CHAPTER II

Bwana Brutus

It was the middle of the night and the boys were not expecting a visitor. Could it be a shipwreck survivor? Frank raised his hand in a signal of caution as the knocks came again, this time even louder.

"Who's there?" he called.

"It is I. William."

Frank stepped forward and flung the door open. "Hi, William. Come on in."

Framed in the entrance stood a tall, well-built black youth, about the same age as the boys from Bayport. He had a handsome face, lit up now by a broad white smile. Like the others, he wore cut-off jeans and a tee shirt. Around his neck dangled a small trinket carved in the shape of an African native.

The boys had met William on the beach shortly after their arrival and had become friends. Joe had developed a special interest in William's hobby of African lore and his great admiration for King Mansa Musa. He had even learned a few words of Swahili, which William was studying.

"Hujambo?" ("How are you?") William asked.

"Sijambo, ahsante," ("I am well, thank you,") Joe replied.

"You learn Swahili fast," William said with a nod as he stepped inside and closed the door behind him. "I came because I feared your house might have been blown down."

"Thanks," Phil said. "The cottage survived but we nearly lost Joe."

"How so? And what do we have here?" The Jamaican boy looked curiously at the mask.

"It's a long story," Joe said.

Spelling one another, the companions told their guest about the lights on the sea, Joe's disappearance, and the discovery of the strange face in the sand.

"Now we're trying to figure out what this mask is all about," Frank concluded. "Have a seat while Phil scrapes off the sea moss."

"Take my place," Chet said, offering William his chair.

"Thank you, Chet. You are very considerate." William spoke with a slow, measured cadence. His English, with a slight British inflection, was perfect.

"I'm just sleepy," Chet said with a yawn. "I want to go to bed. Hey, what's that under your belt?"

"A present for you all," William said. He drew out a plastic-covered paperback book and handed it to Chet. "This is the Swahili word book I was telling you about."

"Oh, great! Thanks," Chet said, and he moved his cot out toward the table in order to catch a little light from the candle. He thumped his pillow into a ball and lay back to read the book.

The others, meanwhile, watched as Phil continued to work on the mask.

"That is a most distinguished face," William said. "Probably the replica of an important man."

The knife blade worked about the eyes. They were blank. The mouth, cleaned of the greenish covering, looked stern and noble. Even the beard seemed patrician, with every curl carefully arranged.

"Wait a sec," Phil said. "You know what? I think this is a death mask. Remember the pictures in our ancient history textbook?"

"You're right," Joe said. "When a famous or rich person died they'd take a plaster impression of the face and make a mask from it."

"Sometimes," William added, "even while the person was living, they would do this."

Phil stopped scraping and looked closely at the treasure.

"A real handsome guy," Tony said. "He looks Italian."

"Maybe a Roman or a Greek," William ventured.

"Let's call him Brutus for the moment," Biff suggested.

"Not bad," Phil said with a smile. He wrinkled his brow in thought. *"Habari za asubuhi, Bwana Brutus."*

"Very good," William said. "Good morning, Mr. Brutus. You are learning fast, Phil."

From the cot came Chet's sleepy voice. "That's nothing. *Nahitaji vigwe vya viatu."*

"What'd he say?" Joe asked.

"I need a pair of shoelaces," William translated. "Chet, your pronunciation is quite acceptable."

But there was no more comment from Chet. The book rested on his chest, which rose and fell rhythmically to the sound of gentle snoring.

The boys were getting sleepier by the minute, but Phil kept on cleaning the mask.

"Now the face looks pretty good," he finally said. "Let's try to dig some of this crud out of the back."

The mud and other detritus came out in big chunks, and soon the mask resembled a hollow shell. When Tony wiped off the last few sandy particles with his handkerchief, he peered intently into the back of the cast. "I think there's some writing here," he said, handing the mask to Joe, who squinted at the odd-looking lettering written in several neat lines. But he could make nothing of it, either.

Phil examined the text. "It looks like Arabic to me," he said. "What do you say, William?"

"You may be right. Did you know the word Swahili is a modified form of the Arabic *sawa-hil,* meaning 'coast people?' "

"You're a walking encyclopedia," Biff said with admiration. "Why the coast people?"

"It was the language of East Africa," William explained, "and it was carried to the interior by traders and missionaries."

When talk swung back to the mysterious mask, Phil said, "We ought to keep it a secret. What say, Frank?"

"Yes, until we learn more about it. I'll hide it in my gear."

"Good idea," Joe agreed. "And now let's call it a night. Will you stay with us, William? We have an extra sleeping bag."

"I would be honored to be your guest."

Frank snuffed out the candle and stretched out on his cot. The last thing he remembered was William telling Phil about Mansa Musa, fabulously rich king of Mali in fourteenth-century West Africa.

The storm abated sometime during the night, and when Frank awoke the next morning, the bright Caribbean sunshine was sifting through the cracks in the shutters. He rose and flung them open, flooding the cottage with daylight. As he shielded his eyes to peer out at the sea, he noted knots of people standing on the beach. They seemed to be talking excitedly.

"Look, guys, something's going on out there!" Frank said as the others rose from their slumber. They dressed quickly and hurried outside.

"Don't you want breakfast first?" Chet asked. "I'm starved."

"You stay and make it," Joe said.

"Okay. How many want eggs, sunny-side up, and bacon?"

All the boys accepted with a good-natured cheer, and Chet padded around the kitchen, searching for the skillet. The others ran to the spectators, who appeared to be looking for something along the shore.

William spoke to a group of Jamaicans, while the Americans mingled with vacationers. Fifteen minutes later they met to exchange information.

"This is the story," William began. "A treasure-hunting ship was wrecked offshore last night. It had found the site of a sunken galleon by radar, and the men were about to dive when the storm struck."

"Were they drowned?" Biff asked.

William shook his head. "That is the miracle. All three survived."

"Pretty rugged, I'd say," Phil commented.

"Their boat is a total loss," William went on. "It broke like matchwood."

"Are the people looking for the pieces?" Tony asked.

"No. Jamaicans who understand the sea think part of the old galleon may have been washed in. They are looking for treasure!"

"Come on, let's join them," Phil said. The boys walked back and forth, eyes glued to the strip where the shiny sand met the lapping surf. Seaweed and odd pieces of debris dotted the sand. Farther down the shore, a girl cried out in surprise and held up an old coin.

"No doubt it is from the galleon," William said.

Minutes later Biff bent down to retrieve another. "Hey, I've got something!" he cried.

His companions crowded around for a look, and others joined them to gaze curiously at the blackened coin, which probably had been buried for centuries.

Three men pushed through to Biff. The oldest, handsome and in his middle thirties, asked to see the find. He turned it over and over, studying it carefully.

"It's authentic," he said. "A Spanish silver piece."

The two other men examined it next. They were younger and rough looking.

"How do you know it's authentic?" Tony asked.

"I'm Tiffany Stribling. These are my assistants, Sam Brown and George Aker. That was our boat that sank last night."

"Oh, you're the treasure hunters," Phil said.

Aker nodded with a one-sided smile. "You know, big boy, you can't keep this. It belongs to the Jamaican government."

"We'll turn it in," Frank said, and added, "What kind of galleon were you looking for?"

This time Brown spoke, his voice edged with condescension. "That's our secret. Why should we tell you amateurs?"

Joe bristled and was about to respond when Chet trotted up to say that breakfast was ready. He caught part of the conversation and blurted, "Amateurs, eh? We've found a——"

Joe stepped on his foot.

"Oh, you found something else?" Stribling said. "What was it?"

CHAPTER III

Three Bad Eggs

TIFFANY's question went unanswered, and his friendly demeanor disappeared suddenly.

"Why all the secrecy?" he demanded. "We're experts and can tell you whether the item you found is worth anything or not."

Frank shook his head. "We prefer to keep it to ourselves."

Aker put on his lopsided smile again. "We can turn you in for concealing Jamaican property!"

"Who says we're concealing anything?" Phil said. "Maybe it was just an old log."

"Don't get smart," Sam Brown said.

Finally Chet pleaded, "Listen guys. Breakfast is ready. If you don't come now, those eggs will taste like scuba flippers!"

They hurried back into the beach house to find their meal still warm enough for total enjoyment. Nothing was said to Chet until they had finished, and he kept looking from one boy to the other until the question finally came.

"Why did you spill the beans, Chet?" Biff demanded. "You didn't have to tell those guys we found the mask."

"I didn't say anything about the mask," Chet protested.

"You indicated we found something."

"Don't scold him," Frank said. "Remember, he was asleep when we decided to keep this a secret."

"Thanks," Chet said. "Frank, you want some more eggs?"

The boys laughed and Joe said, "Don't forget, Chet, button your lip from now on, okay?"

William had been silent for a while, but when he finished his coffee he put down the cup and said, "I think there may be trouble ahead."

"You mean those men?" Tony asked.

"They looked like ruffians to me! Jamaicans do not like that kind of treasure hunter working off our shores."

"They were pretty high-handed," Phil agreed.

"Let's find out everything we can about the mask today," Frank suggested. "I noticed a museum next to the post office."

"It is a good one, too," William said. "The museum has a fine collection of shipwreck relics and old records."

"Will you go with us?" Joe asked.

"I wish to be excused," the Jamaican said. "I promised my grandfather to visit him today. He lives a way up the beach from here."

"Okay. Will we see you later?"

"Of course. Since you are leaving for home tomorrow, I would like to spend as much time with you as possible."

"William, can I go with you?" Chet asked. You told me about your grandfather and I'd like to meet him."

"Certainly. He will be delighted. But I suggest that we find a better hiding place for that mask before we all leave."

They looked around until Tony located two loose floorboards in the kitchenette near the sink. Frank and Joe pried them up enough to slip the mask underneath.

Chet and William lingered to finish the chores while the others walked along the beach. Half a mile farther on, they headed inland until they reached the center of town. The streets were narrow and lined with shops catering to the tourist trade.

Main Street gave onto a small park dominated at one end by an ancient cannon. To the right were the municipal buildings. The Bayporters went straight to the museum. After they explained their mission to the curator, an intense middle-aged woman, she took a great interest in the Americans.

"So many ships were sunk off Jamaica," she said. "English, Spanish, Dutch. And many lives were lost."

"Were there any Arab ships?" asked Joe.

The woman thought for a moment. "No. But I do recall that a Portuguese slave ship, the *Africanus Rex*, was lost some time in the early seventeenth century. It carried an Arab Barbary crew."

The curator added with a smile, "It's interesting that you should mention this, because some of the slaves escaped to shore and became free men." She glanced over Frank's shoulder. "Is that man looking for you?"

The Hardys whirled to see George Aker's back as he tried to slip out unobserved.

"Quick, keep a tail on him, Phil," Frank said. "Biff, Tony, you help out, too."

The boys dashed out while the Hardys thanked the curator for her assistance.

"You've really given us quite a bit of help," Joe said. "By the way, is anything known about a death mask lost on one of your beaches?"

"I never heard of anything like that."

Frank and Joe hurried from the museum. Partway down the block they noticed Biff stationed at the corner. When they caught up with him, he said, "Come on. Tony's down the next street. I think he knows where Phil went."

They turned right and passed a number of shops. Then they saw Tony beckoning. "Phil's on

Aker's trail. He's standing in that doorway. See?"

The boys turned left this time and walked in single file close to the store fronts. They arrived at the spot where Phil had concealed himself.

"Aker met the other two guys," Phil reported, "and they went into that restaurant two doors down."

"Stribling and his boys are very much interested in us," Joe said. "Too interested to suit me."

"I wonder what their game is." Phil said.

"If we could eavesdrop, we might find out," said Frank.

"But how?" Phil asked.

"You stay here while Joe and I reconnoiter."

Just then a boy about ten years old walked past, and Frank reached out to touch his arm. When he stopped, Frank asked, "Would you like to earn a dollar?"

"Yes, sir!"

Frank took a single from his wallet. "Here's what you have to do. Walk to that restaurant and look through the window. See if three men are sitting together, and tell me just where their table is located."

"That's easy," the boy said. He took the money and skipped down the street. He peered into the window, shading his eyes against the reflection of the glass. Then he turned and hurried back. "There are no men that I could see."

"None at all?"

"No. But there are booths in the back," their young spy went on, "and the waiter was serving somebody. I could not see who it was."

"Wait a minute," Frank said. "Did the waiter serve the food to the booth closest to the window or farther back?"

"The first one," the boy said.

"Okay. You did a good job."

The Jamaican smiled brightly and hurried off.

Biff said, "Now what?"

Frank mulled his strategy for a moment. "If we walk in the front door and try to listen, they'll spot us."

"What about the back way?" Joe suggested.

"That'll have to be it. But we'd better not all go in. Just one."

The Hardys looked at Phil.

"You mean I'm elected?" the boy asked.

"Unanimously," Frank said. "You're good at this kind of thing. Find the back door; then slip into the booth next to Stribling and his crew."

"Will do, skipper. Where shall we meet?"

"In the park," Frank replied.

Phil started off. He turned into an alley until he reached a narrow lane behind the buildings. He found the back of the eating place easily enough. Garbage cans stood filled to the brim, and, as he passed them, a cat jumped out of one and scampered off.

Phil entered the kitchen through the screen

door, but a huge black man with a chef's cap blocked his way. "You can't come in this way, man! Go around front!"

Phil looked at him pleadingly and spoke several sentences of gibberish.

A smile crossed the cook's face. "You don't speak English?"

Phil pointed to his mouth, indicating that he was hungry.

"I never heard any language like that," the Jamaican said.

Phil uttered more gibberish, and the man pointed to the swinging door leading into the restaurant.

Phil went in quietly, staying close to the right wall, and slid into the second booth. He could hear the men talking. Just then a waiter appeared with the menu.

"Cook says you don't speak English," the man said, and ran his finger down the day's offering. Phil pointed to chicken soup and grinned. It was brought to him immediately, along with some biscuits.

Phil remained quiet, listening carefully for telltale information. The men spoke in low voices, and the hum of an air conditioner nearly drowned out their words. Finally Phil heard something.

"Rex," Tiffany was saying.

"Yes, Tip," came Brown's voice. "That's right."

There was some mumbling, then Stribling again, "What do you think, George?"

Aker said, "The Hardys. They rented the place. Later on——"

Phil could not make out the rest. The men stood up and walked out of the restaurant.

The boy left his soup, beckoned to the waiter for the check, paid, and hurried through the kitchen again.

The chef's eyes grew large with surprise. "I don't know what country you come from," he muttered, "but they have funny customs, man!"

Phil dodged between the garbage cans, ran up the alley, and hurried to the park. The others were waiting, and he quickly repeated everything he had heard. When he gave a sample of his "foreign language," the boys laughed.

"That was a good trick," Joe said.

"I want to learn more about this gang," Frank said. "There must be a newspaper in town that can help us."

By asking a policeman for directions, the boys found the small office of the *Gazette* without any difficulty. It smelled of ink and paper.

Frank asked for the city editor and was directed to a cubicle along one wall. A black man was typing. The nameplate on his desk read, "James Douglas."

"Hi, Mr. Douglas," Frank said. He then introduced himself.

The newsman swiveled around. "What can I do for you?"

Frank told him about the treasure hunters and explained that he and his friends would like some additional information, if possible.

Douglas smiled. "Those three have quite a history. They've looked for treasure in several parts of the world." He named various places, including Africa.

"Do they have a good reputation?" Phil inquired.

"I won't speak against any man," the editor said. "But I would advise you not to associate with them."

"You mean they're criminals?" Tony prodded.

"They have not been in jail in Jamaica. But in your country—you might call them bad eggs."

"We get the picture. Thanks, Mr. Douglas."

The boys stepped outside. "I've got the uncomfortable feeling that our mask is in jeopardy," Phil said. "Let's go back to the cottage."

"Can we stop at the post office on the way?" Joe asked. "Maybe we've got some mail from home."

Their family had promised to write in care of General Delivery, and much to their delight several letters were waiting for the Hardys.

One of them was in Aunt Gertrude's handwriting. Frank opened the letter. "Listen to this, Joe," he said. " 'Nothing good can come of going so far from home. Keep your hands on your wallets. You never can tell when foreigners pick your pockets!' "

Frank rocked with laughter, then continued. " 'Beware of strangers. They can only lead to trouble.' "

"Good old Aunty," Joe said. "She's always worried about us."

"She may be right, warning about strangers," Phil said with a grin.

As they walked on, Frank opened a letter from his father. After scanning it, he said, "Dad's on a new case. A multimillion-dollar racket involving the theft of airline tickets."

"I read something about that," Tony said. "Now you'll probably go back and dig into a brand-new mystery."

"I think we have one right here," Biff said, as the boys jogged to the waterfront.

"Boy, could I go for a swim," Tony said.

"You can, as soon as we get back," Phil told him.

When the Bayporters reached their beach house and stepped through the door, Joe emitted a cry of despair. The place was a mess. Everything had been ransacked!

"Good grief!" Frank exclaimed. He ran to the kitchenette and pried up the floorboards.

The mask was gone!

CHAPTER IV

An Ancient Legend

"OH, nuts!" Biff said. "We should have taken *Bwana* Brutus with us, or left Chet to guard the place."

"It's too late to moan over it now," Joe said, "and perfectly obvious who the thieves are. We have to find them!"

The area was quickly scouted for footprints. Besides their own tracks in the sand, the boys discovered evidence that the beach house had been circled several times. There were deep depressions in the sand beneath the windows, indicating that the prowlers might have stood on their toes to look inside.

"See. Here the tracks lead along the beach," Tony said. "They shouldn't be hard to follow."

"Tip and his gang are too smart for that," Frank said. "But let's check 'em."

The trail was clear for several hundred yards.

Then, abruptly, it took a right-angle turn and disappeared into the surf.

"You were right, Frank," Phil said. "Who knows how far these crooks walked in the water?"

They scanned the shore for another quarter mile with no success. Then Joe shifted his gaze inland to a grove of palms, where a darting movement had caught his eye.

"Look!" he said. "I think somebody's hiding behind those trees!"

Biff's long legs carried him across the sand first to the fringe of palms. The others were close on his heels, when a man stepped out from behind a triple clump.

"Sam Brown!" Biff exploded. He leaped forward and grasped the surprised Brown by the shirt front.

"Wait!" Frank cautioned.

But Biff was in no mood for prudence. He shook Sam, whose head bobbed back and forth as he protested with curses.

"Give back that mask!" Biff boomed.

By this time Frank and Joe had pried Sam loose from their buddy's clutches.

"Cool it," Frank advised, "before you snap his head off."

Sam stepped back and scowled. "Oh, so that's what you found on the beach! Thanks for telling me. But I don't have your mask. Keep your hands off me and go play Halloween somewhere else!"

As he spoke, Stribling and Aker appeared from a tangle of sea grapes. The latter rushed up to Biff and swung a right-hand punch.

Biff blocked it and countered with a stiff blow to the chest that sent the man sprawling. At once a free-for-all ensued. It lasted several minutes before Stribling yelled out, "Hey! What are we fighting about?"

"I'll tell you!" Joe stormed. "You ransacked our place and stole something!"

"Stole what?"

"A mask of some sort," Brown said.

"Well, now. That's interesting." Stribling flashed his smile again. "Can you be more specific, please? If we're charged with theft, it's only fair that we know the particulars."

The Bayporters stood there, uncomfortable. Stribling had a way of putting them down. What if he had not taken the mask? Frank and Joe knew that without solid proof of burglary it would be useless to press the issue.

"I think you know all about the particulars," Frank declared.

"Anything you say," the man retorted mockingly.

Then Aker added, "Any more of this physical stuff and you'll regret it!"

Frank turned to his companions. "Okay. Let's break it up." They walked back toward their cottage.

"What'll we do now?" Phil asked as they strode along.

"There are several things we could do," Frank said, his brow furrowed. "Number one, go to the police. They might listen, since these men have shady reputations. But there's a problem. Do we own *Bwana* Brutus or don't we?"

"That's debatable," Phil said.

"Number two. We could put a tail on the gang. If they have the mask they'll probably do something with it. But we're stymied here, too. Our plane leaves tomorrow, so that doesn't give us much time."

"Kind of hopeless, isn't it?" Biff said.

Nobody answered, and they walked on in silence. Chet and William had not yet returned when they reached the beach house.

"So who's for a swim?" Tony said brightly, trying to dispel the pall of defeat.

Joe managed a smile. "Okay, maybe it'll cool Biff off."

Minutes later all were in the sea. Tony and Frank wore snorkel gear and splashed along in shallow water, enjoying the myriad colors of marine life.

After a while Joe tapped his shoulder and Frank looked up. "What's the matter?"

"Here come Chet and William."

Far down the beach they could make out the pair. William, tall and lithe; Chet, block-solid, with a rocking gait. Between the boys and supporting himself with a cane, walked an elderly, gray-haired black man.

The Hardys called to their friends and all swam ashore. It was then that they noticed that William was carrying a brown paper bag.

"I'm glad you brought lunch!" Phil joked.

William looked at Chet and smiled. Then he introduced his grandfather. The boys shook his hand, rough-skinned and firm from a lifetime of hard work.

"Glad to meet you, Granddad," Frank said. "We're having a lot of fun with William. Wish we could stay longer on your island." Then he turned to the Jamaican boy and Chet.

"The mask is gone! Those devils stole it while we were in town!"

"No, man," William replied. *"Bwana* Brutus is right here—in this bag!"

"What?"

The Americans crowded around as he opened the top of the sack. "See? You did not have to worry."

"Worry!" Joe blurted. "When we saw it was gone we set off after Stribling and company like the Marines! What happened?"

"It is quite simple," William said. "After you left this morning, Chet and I noticed Stribling and his friends heading this way."

"They were walking very slowly," Chet added, "and they kept looking around."

"So we guessed that they were coming to search for *Bwana* Brutus," William concluded.

"What did you do?"

"We got him out from under the floor, slipped out the back door, and took off!"

"I wanted to fight them," Chet said.

"But I dislike violence," William commented. "So we did it the easy way."

"That's using your head," Biff said with a chuckle. "Good thing you weren't with us," and he briefly related the details of the brush with the gang.

"Which proves what Dad has told us many times," Frank said. "Never jump to conclusions."

"Yes," William agreed. "A wise course of action."

While they spoke, the old man listened intently and smiled, evidently pleased with his grandson's new friends.

"Let's go inside for some chow," Joe finally suggested.

"I'm all for it," Chet added. "We have fixin's for sandwiches in the cottage."

While they lingered over lunch, conversation eddied about the strange mask. How long had it lain in the sand? What did the cryptic writing say? Why were the treasure hunters so interested in it?

"Grandfather may have a clue," William said. *"Babu,* tell them what you told Chet and me."

The old man, who had finished eating, pushed his chair back from the table and rested his hands on the crook of the cane. His voice, high-pitched with age, was clear and expressive. He spoke slowly.

"There is a legend, passed down many years from my grandfather's grandfather's grandfather."

"Is it a true story?" asked Phil.

"Maybe not."

"Go ahead," William coaxed.

"It is about a ship called the *Africanus Rex.* My ancestors were on it. It had a treasure. It was neither gold, nor silver, nor gems, but a secret kept in the captain's cabin. Anyone who dared look was——" He moved a forefinger across his throat.

"Life was cheap then," William said.

"Say, do you suppose the mask has something to do with that treasure?" Frank asked.

The old man shrugged. "Perhaps."

"I'll bet the galleon the treasure hunters were looking for was the *Africanus Rex!*" Biff declared.

Frank turned to William. "Do you or your grandfather know anybody in town who can read Arabic?"

"Oh, yes," William replied. "Ali El Ansari does."

"Who's he?"

The boys were told that Ali El Ansari was a merchant, originally from Cairo. He ran a curio shop that contained a large collection of African objects.

"I visit him often," William said. "He might be able to help us."

The grandfather excused himself and said good-by. He went home while the boys hastened to town.

Ali El Ansari's shop, they found, was only several doors down from the restaurant where Phil had spoken gibberish to gain entrance.

"Behave yourself now and speak nicely," Frank said, nudging his friend.

"Okay, Dad," Phil quipped.

The store interior was postage-stamp size. A single counter faced the door, and glass cases extended from floor to ceiling on either side. When William tapped a hand bell on the counter, footsteps sounded from inside, and a slender man in his thirties appeared. He had high cheek bones, black curly hair, and a tan complexion, which, with his neat dark business suit, gave him a somber appearance.

When he saw William, he greeted him with a subdued smile. "Good afternoon, my friend. What can I do for you today?"

"I have something to show you, sir," William said, pulling the mask out of the brown bag. The man leaned on the counter on his elbows and held the metal object, turning it from one side to the other. Then he looked up.

"This is a rare find. Where did you get it?"

"On the beach," Joe said.

"It is very old and valuable," El Ansari said.

"Is it a death mask?" Phil asked.

"I believe so."

"What we would like to know about," Frank said, "is the writing on the inside. Is it Arabic?"

"Indeed, yes. Let me get my magnifier." The man went into the back and returned with a thick lens, which he put to his eye.

After studying the inscription for a while, he translated, " 'He who does not travel will not know the value of men.' That is a Moorish proverb. The person who owned this probably was educated and well-traveled."

Then Ali El Ansari said, "There is more here. It is visible only under my glass."

"What is it?" Frank asked eagerly.

"A compass. This is curious."

The man concentrated on the new discovery. Finally he said, "At the South point of the compass is the word 'gold,' at the North, the word 'salt.' And beneath the compass it says, 'Mysterious Caravan!' "

CHAPTER V

An Ominous Telegram

JOE Hardy let out a low whistle. "Mysterious caravan! What could that possibly mean?"

"It means you're into another mystery. What else?" Chet said. "Anything unusual about that?"

The others laughed while Frank jotted down the words on a piece of paper, and put it in his wallet.

The Arab said, "Would you consider selling this piece?"

"You know we can't," Frank said. "It belongs to the government of Jamaica."

The man stroked his chin thoughtfully and replied, "Not necessarily. Who is to say it came from the sea? Perhaps somebody lost it in the sand years ago."

"You should have seen the moss and barnacles we scraped off it," William said. "It came from that old wreck all right."

"In that case," Ali said with a bow, "I abide by your decision."

The Hardys thanked the shopkeeper and the boys returned to the beach house for their last full day of sun and fun on the island. But the cottage was never left unattended. One of them remained there at all times, guarding the treasure, while the others enjoyed snorkeling and skin-diving.

William left for his own home shortly after supper. The night was starlit, with tropical soft-ness in the air. Much to the surprise of the Hardys, they were not disturbed by prowlers. The next morning Tony Prito said, "How do you like that for a peaceful sleep? Stribling and his boys must have given up."

But they found out soon that this was not the case. William raced up the beach and burst in to greet his friends. He was breathing hard from the long run.

"Did you hear about Ali?" he asked.

"No. What happened?" Frank said.

"They got to him last night. Three men wear-ing stocking masks beat him up. He is in the hospital now."

"Did they rob his place?" Phil asked.

"That is the strange part of it. The shop was thoroughly ransacked, but nothing was taken. They were looking for *Bwana* Brutus!"

"How do you know?" Joe asked.

"Ali reported to the police that the men demanded the mask the Hardy boys had 'sold him.'"

"You mean he got beaten up on our account?" Frank said. "What a shame! Stribling's goons must have seen us enter the shop."

"We owe him something," Tony Prito stated. "Let's all go to the hospital and visit him."

The boys readily agreed and decided to take him a present.

"We'll stop in town and buy something," Joe said.

"What about the mask?" Phil wanted to know. "We shouldn't leave it here."

"Don't worry. I'm taking care of that right now," Joe replied. He removed the equipment from his camera case and inserted the death mask.

"Old Brutus is going with us," he declared.

On the way to the hospital they stopped at a florist's to get a bouquet for the injured man. When they entered the Arab's room, they were stunned by his condition. Ali's head was swathed in a broad bandage. His right eye was blackened, and his left arm, immobile and in a cast, lay on the sheet. A nurse had cautioned the boys not to stay long.

After conveying their regrets, they prepared to leave. Ali smiled wanly and whispered, "Be very careful. That mask must be of fabulous value. Do you still have it?"

Joe patted the leather camera case.

"Get rid of it as soon as you can. Your lives are in danger!"

The boys said good-by and returned to the cottage, where the chore of packing began.

"Listen, Joe," Frank said. "I was about to ask you the other day. What happened to my other pair of shorts?"

"Don't look at me!" Joe said with mock hurt. "I wear only one pair at a time."

"Chet?"

"They wouldn't fit me," the chubby boy said, and Tony, Phil, and Biff claimed they had not seen them either.

When the suitcases were filled, Frank threw his sport jacket over his arm. The thought flashed through his mind that he had not worn it once since removing it from his bag the day they arrived.

"Everyone ready to go?" he asked.

They all were. William would accompany his friends to the airport for the final good-by. Before they left, he removed the trinket from around his neck and handed it to Joe.

"Here, this is a gift to you," he said. "A keepsake of friendship."

"But I can't accept that," Joe said, embarrassed by the generous offer. "It's some kind of an heirloom, isn't it?"

"Please," William said. "I know we'll always be good friends."

Their eyes met for a few silent seconds, then Joe smiled. He took the gift and put the chain over his head. "William, you're a great guy!"

Carrying their bags, the boys trekked into town. "We'll drop the mask off at police headquarters," Frank said.

"Take this silver coin, too," Biff said.

"There is a cab," William spoke up. "Shall I hold it? It is already late and we need two."

"Tell you what," Frank said. "Why don't you go ahead, while Joe and I take care of the mask. That'll give you more time to check in. Take our bags, too, and we'll meet you at the airport later."

"Okay," Phil said, and the four piled into the taxi. Joe and Frank walked toward the municipal buildings. They were halfway down the block when they heard rapid footsteps behind them. Whirling around, they saw Sam Brown, George Aker, and another man.

"Wait a minute," Aker called out. "What's your hurry?"

The men's ploy was obvious. "Let's split and run," Frank said. "We'll meet at the airport."

"Roger."

The boys dashed off, Frank running across the street, Joe straight ahead toward police headquarters.

There shouldn't be any problem, Joe thought, of reaching the police before the pursuers, one of whom had followed Frank.

But he had taken no more than twenty steps when Stribling and an unkempt-looking fellow approached him from the opposite direction, trying to block his path!

Joe raced into the street, just missing a car that screeched to a halt to avoid him. As he gained the other side, he tripped on the curb and fell, sprawled out on the sidewalk. Quickly he picked himself up, grabbed the camera case, and dashed away while onlookers stared at the chase. "Not a cop in sight!" Joe thought desperately. "What'll I do?"

As the men gained on him, he saw the restaurant where Phil had eavesdropped. He ducked into an alley, went around behind the place, and burst into the kitchen, nearly bowling over the big chef.

"Help me!" Joe gasped. "Please!"

The Jamaican grabbed his shirt front. At the same time his eyes fell on the African trinket around Joe's neck.

"Where did you get this?"

"William Ellis gave it to me."

Without another word the chef shoved him into the pantry and barred the back door with arms akimbo.

Joe's pursuers were now looking behind garbage cans, peering into every doorway.

"Did you see a white kid hanging around here?" Stribling asked the cook.

"We'll meet at the airport!" Frank said.

He looked impassively at the questioner. "Listen, man, I mind my own business. But if you spill one of those cans, I'll put it on your head like an Easter bonnet."

The men hurried off, cursing their bad luck. When they were safely out of sight, the chef opened the pantry door. "What they want with you, man?"

"They're thieves. Tried to take my camera case."

"Well, they're gone now."

"Could you call a taxi for me, please?" Joe said.

The big man went to the telephone in the restaurant and a few minutes later a cab appeared in front of the place. Joe said good-by with a look of gratitude on his face.

"If you're a friend of William's, you're a friend of mine," the Jamaican said, with a big grin.

The taxi sped toward the airport.

In the meantime, Frank had already arrived and told the others what had happened.

"I figured I could make them run after me instead of Joe," he said. "But I guessed wrong."

"I hope nothing happened to him," Phil said. "We shouldn't have left you the way we did."

Their flight was called and passengers filed from the waiting room through the final gate.

"Please don't leave till my brother Joe arrives," Frank said to the agent who checked the boarding passes.

"We'll hold it as long as we can," the man replied.

Soon the plane was filled. "I'll have to close the gate now," the official said. "Do you want to take another flight?"

"I think we'll have to—oh, there he is!" Joe hurried up to them, the camera case swinging in his right hand.

"Just in time," Frank said.

"Kwa heri," William said. "Good-by to all of you!"

The boys shook hands and invited William to visit them in Bayport whenever he could. Then they hurried through the gate and onto the plane.

Once aboard, Frank handed his sport jacket to a stewardess, asking her to hang it up. Something white fluttered to the floor. She picked it up.

"Does this underwear belong to you?" she asked.

A dozen heads turned and the boys laughed out loud.

"Your missing shorts!" Joe snorted, sliding into his seat. "And you blamed me! Some nerve!"

"They must have gotten stuck inside my jacket in the suitcase," Frank said lamely. "But now tell us. What happened to you?"

Joe described his escape. "William's trinket saved me," he concluded. "It must have a special meaning."

"And you still have the mask?"

"Right here in my camera case."

"Now you're carrying contraband," Phil declared.

"We'll just have to take it along," Frank said. "Nothing we can do about it."

The flight north was smooth and they enjoyed a good lunch. In New York they changed planes and arrived in Bayport without further excitement. Their parents were on hand to meet them, and they went their separate ways.

At the Hardy home, after their aunt greeted them, she handed them a telegram. Frank ripped it open.

"It's from William! Listen: 'George Aker took the second section of that flight to New York. He is on your trail.'"

The boys told Aunt Gertrude and their parents what had happened, and Mr. Hardy immediately turned on the electronic surveillance system that protected their home.

Then Joe pulled the mask out of his camera case. Aunt Gertrude shuddered. "How horrible!" she exclaimed. "A death mask. This can bring nothing but bad luck. Look at those eyes! It just gives me the willies!"

"It won't bite you," Joe said with a grin.

"Worse than that," Aunt Gertrude said. "It's going to haunt us!"

Later in the evening, Mr. Hardy called his sons into his study. He was a handsome man, graying slightly at the temples. His face was rugged, his shoulders square, and his general demeanor confident. Fenton Hardy had once been a top-ranking detective with the New York Police Department, but had retired to Bayport to raise his family and conduct a private-investigation service that had gained a world-wide reputation.

He sat behind his desk as Frank and Joe slumped into lounge chairs.

"I think you had quite some excitement," Mr. Hardy said.

"You can say that again," Joe replied, adding, "can you tell us anything about your new case?"

His father explained that he had been commissioned to work for a number of airlines, acting together. "It's a pretty serious situation," he said. "Carriers are losing millions of dollars in ticket thefts. Previously, a few had been stolen by employees every now and then, but now a wholesale pilferage is going on. Cartons of blanks are hijacked from printing plants and wind up in the hands of a crooked network. They even went as far as demanding ransom for the blanks!"

"It wasn't paid, was it?" Joe asked.

"It was. One airline paid seventy-thousand dollars for tickets that could have been worth two million. This must be stopped and the airlines are going all out to——"

A shrill noise interrupted the detective. The alarm!

All three rushed to the door. Aunt Gertrude screamed that her prediction had come true. The "intruder," however, was Biff Hooper. He walked briskly up the front steps.

"Hey, it's only me!" he said. "I was driving by and noticed someone snooping around. Thought you'd like to know."

"I wouldn't be surprised if it was Aker," Frank said.

"Aker?" Biff asked. "He's in Jamaica!"

"Not any more." Frank showed his friend William's telegram.

"Wow!" Biff said. "You must really have hit on something with that mask."

"No doubt it holds a clue that the crooks know about and we don't," Frank said. "I'm sure they wouldn't go to those lengths for just a piece of metal, even if it is an antique."

The Hardys notified the police immediately, then started a search themselves.

"Frank, you check the shrubs on the other side of the house," Mr. Hardy said. "Joe and Biff, try the back. I'll look across the street."

They rushed out the door and split up. Frank walked through remnants of snow to a dark clump of mountain laurel. As he was about to peer into the shadows, a figure jumped out and clapped a crushing headlock on him!

Frank tried to cry out, but in vain!

CHAPTER VI

Bug on the Window

FRANK struggled with his assailant, but could not break the deadly grip. He felt the man's muscles flexing as he applied more pressure to the headlock. Spots began to swim before the boy's eyes, and he knew that he was in danger of passing out.

With one final wrench Frank broke loose from the vise and fell to the ground while the intruder ran toward the street. Moments later, Frank heard the sound of a motor revving up and a car making a fast getaway.

Frank rested on hands and knees until his head cleared, then struggled to his feet and called for help.

Joe and Biff raced over to him to hear what happened.

"We'll chase that scoundrel!" Biff declared, racing to his car with Joe at his heels. But it was a futile effort. The intruder was long out of sight, and minutes later the two boys returned.

Meanwhile, the police had arrived and were searching the grounds. The only clue was footprints between the mountain laurels and the first-floor windows.

"It was Aker. I feel sure of that," Frank said. He told his father about the man's sturdy build. "Powerful arms, as I recall," he concluded.

At breakfast the next day Fenton Hardy announced that he and Sam Radley, his assistant, were leaving town for a few days to investigate the airline-ticket racket.

"There's a printing outfit in Connecticut," the detective explained, "that supplies blanks to several airlines. A truck from this plant was hijacked, and the thieves stole thousands of tickets."

"Sounds like an inside job," Frank said.

"That's what we think. Sam and I will give the place a thorough check to see if any employees are involved."

"Can we help you, Dad?" Joe asked.

"Later, perhaps," Mr. Hardy replied. "So far Sam and I can handle this alone."

Frank and Joe decided to go to the local library to look up African history. Perhaps they would find a clue to the gold–salt reference carved into the back of the mask.

Half a dozen volumes were available, but the

librarian recommended one title in particular, *The Golden Trade of the Moors.*

Frank obtained it and they walked into the hushed and carpeted reading room. Sitting side-by-side, they pored over the events in North and West Africa from the fourteenth century on.

"Look, here's something about Mansa Musa, King of Mali," Joe pointed out. "No wonder William admired him so much."

Their excited voices could be heard by one of the librarians. She looked up and cautioned them to speak lower. They nodded in embarrassment and quietly devoured the pages devoted to the fabulous Mansa Musa.

The black king, who was a Muslim, set out on a *hadj,* or pilgrimage, to Mecca in 1324. Mounted on horseback, he was preceded by five-hundred slaves. Each slave carried a staff of gold weighing five hundred *mithqual.* A footnote explained that a *mithqual,* or *mithkal,* was about one-eighth of an ounce of gold. They proceeded in a camel caravan numbering nearly one-thousand camels.

"Holy catfish!" Joe whispered. "Can you imagine what that's worth at today's prices?"

When the king passed through Cairo, he gave away so much gold as gifts that the country was thrown into a terrible inflation that lasted many years.

"What a guy," Frank said.

The report went on to say that Mansa Musa was a good, just king, greatly loved by his subjects.

"Do you know how far that trip was?" Frank asked. "Let's look it up on the map."

"Wow! On foot and with camels? It seems impossible."

Joe went through the indexes of the remaining books and finally said, "Frank, look at this. Salt was carried south from Sijilmasa and exchanged for equal weights of gold in West Africa! That's what the inscription on the mask refers to."

Further reading told them that Sijilmasa had long since become a lost city.

"Perhaps that's where the mysterious caravan vanished," Frank conjectured.

The hours had flown by quickly, and it was noon before the Hardys realized it.

"We'd better get home for lunch," Joe said. "My stomach's growling."

"Mine, too."

The boys arrived to find their mother and Aunt Gertrude in a state of excitement.

"You've had a phone call," Mrs. Hardy said, "from Jamaica!"

The brothers looked at each other in amazement.

"Who was it?" Frank asked.

"Your friend William. He wants you to call him back right away."

Mrs. Hardy handed Frank the number, and he had no difficulty reaching William.

"Hi, this is Frank Hardy. What's going on down there?"

Frank listened for more than a minute, then said. "Sure. That's fine. You let us know and we'll meet you at the airport."

After Frank hung up, the others were eager to hear the news.

"Is he coming to visit us?" Mrs. Hardy asked.

"Yes. He shadowed Stribling and Brown and found out that they want to get the mask at any cost. They're leaving Jamaica for New York tomorrow morning. Whether they'll come on to Bayport, William doesn't know."

"Our buddy's really on the ball!" Joe said with admiration.

"Sure is. He'll take the same flight and follow them wherever they go. He'll call us from New York and let us know what's up."

"My goodness, that's very dangerous!" Aunt Gertrude said. "He should stay in Jamaica. What if those terrible cutthroats come to Bayport?"

"We'll take care of them!" Joe vowed.

"It also solves the problem of the mask," Frank said. "William can take it back to Jamaica when he leaves."

"And it'll give us more time to study it," Joe added.

"Right. By the way, Ali's back in his shop and feeling much better."

After lunch Joe said, "You know, Frank, I think Callie and Iola would get a great charge out of this mask. Why don't we invite them over? They can help us polish it."

"Good idea."

Iola Morton, Chet's sister, dated Joe, while Callie Shaw was Frank's favorite girl. When Frank phoned the Morton farm, Callie was there and both accepted the invitation readily. Iola said, "Chet's coming to see you later this afternoon anyway. We'll drive over with him."

"And stay for supper, okay?" Frank asked, raising his eyebrows and nodding to his mother.

Mrs. Hardy smiled a quiet consent. She, too, was fond of the girls.

When Aunt Gertrude heard the news, she bustled about the kitchen to make Chet a pie. His appetite was usually appeased by Aunt Gertrude's goodies, and he praised her cooking all over Bayport and its environs.

At four o'clock a few heavy backfires announced the arrival of Chet's jalopy. The girls were bundled up in ski jackets, and their faces were bright and rosy from the cold air as they entered the Hardys' living room. Chet followed, a bright-yellow skating cap perched on his head.

"I wish I were back in Jamaica," he said. "How

would you like to swim in that warm surf today, Joe?"

Callie and Iola were intrigued by the mask, and after a delicious supper suggested that Frank and Joe drive them back to the Morton farm, where Iola had a special cleaning fluid.

"It'll make *Bwana* Brutus's face shine," Iola said. All agreed, and by seven-thirty were on their way to Chet's place, snow tires humming against the highway.

Frank and Joe kept looking behind to see if anyone was tailing them. Several cars passed, but far back, dim headlights seemed to be holding their position.

"You think that's someone following us?" asked Iola.

"It's probably Chet," Frank said. "He left with us but dropped off the pace."

Conversation turned to winter sports. Skiing had not been good, but the ice skating was the best in years.

"Our pond's like glass," Iola said. "Why don't we have a skating party soon?"

"Fine with us," Joe said as they pulled into the long driveway on the Morton farm. Chet arrived a few minutes later.

It was not until the mask lay on sheets of newspaper on the kitchen table and the girls, using cotton-tipped swabs, were cleaning every crevice in the beard, that the Hardys told them about William's plan to visit.

"You'll like him," Joe said. "He's tops."

"Listen!" Callie said suddenly.

"What is it?"

"I thought I heard a little tap on the window."

None of the others had, but nevertheless the Hardys and Chet hurried out into the biting cold to look around. No one was in sight.

When they were back inside with the girls, Iola inquired, "When is William coming?"

"He's leaving on the nine fifteen A.M. flight to New York tomorrow morning, and will call us when he arrives."

"Maybe he can teach you Swahili," Chet said, looking at the girls. "And I'm warning you. It's not easy!"

Everyone laughed; then Iola held up the mask. The face seemed to be more expressive than ever. Tilted at a certain angle, the mouth even appeared to have a faint smile.

"I still think it's spooky," Chet said.

Later, when the boys got ready to leave, Frank said, "It looks like old Brutus here had a real good beauty treatment." He thanked the girls and offered Callie a ride home.

Just then Chet glanced out the window, which offered a view of the country road that curved around the farm.

"Look at this, guys," he said. "A car just

turned on its lights. It must have been parked."

The Hardys became apprehensive. Why would a car be standing there at this time of night? Frank had a hunch, which he hardly dared think about. "Callie," he said, "which window did you hear that noise at?"

She pointed to the one nearest the kitchen table. After putting on their coats, the Hardys went outside. They scanned every bit of the glass. *Suddenly Frank saw it!*

Far in the left-hand corner was a tiny suction disk. Attached to it was a small matchbox-size instrument and a long, trailing wire.

"The place has been bugged!" Frank cried out.

"You know what that means?" Joe said. "Someone in that car heard our conversation about William!"

"What'll we do now?" Chet asked.

"Get in touch with William and map out an alternate strategy," Frank said.

Both boys were glum as they dropped Callie off. "Cheer up," she said. "Things can't be that bad!"

"You win an Oscar for optimism," Joe said.

When the Hardys arrived home, they telephoned William. But there was no answer.

"I hope we reach him before his flight leaves tomorrow morning," Joe said, worried.

They tried every hour all night long, but to no avail.

"Maybe he's staying with his grandfather," Joe said. "And we don't even know his name. It's his mother's father."

The next day the boys waited for a call from New York. The minutes ticked by in silence. Neither boy spoke much, and they picked sparingly at the food on their plates.

Mrs. Hardy tried to cheer them with no results.

Finally, late in the evening, the phone rang. Joe ran to pick it up. A look of horror came over his face as he listened to the voice on the other end.

"Give us that mask if you want to see William alive again!" a man rasped.

CHAPTER VII

Frank's Brainstorm

THE caller hung up, leaving Joe holding the receiver.

"They've got William!" he finally burst out.

"How terrible!" Aunt Gertrude wailed. "I told you to have nothing to do with strangers! If you took my advice, you wouldn't get into these horrid situations."

"It's not the boys' fault," their mother defended them. She turned to Frank. "Could it be just an empty threat? Maybe these people are only bluffing."

The phone rang again. This time Aunt Gertrude snatched up the receiver. The voice on the other end was loud enough to be heard by the others.

"I mean business!"

"So do I!" Aunt Gertrude berated. "You villains leave my nephews alone or I'll—— I'll——"

Click! The caller hung up.

"Those ruffians make me furious!" The woman huffed.

"You'll never get anywhere talking like that!" Frank said. "We must be calm and find a way to trick them."

"Whoever it is, he'll phone again," was Joe's guess. "We can't turn over the mask without knowing when, where, and how."

The bell sounded once more and Frank took the call. The voice said, "We're not going to give you more than a couple of days to decide."

"We get the message," Frank said evenly. "And we don't want anything to happen to William. How soon shall we make the exchange?"

"I'll contact you tomorrow. We'll discuss details then."

Realizing it was impossible to trace the call, Frank and Joe immediately set off on another tack. First Joe telephoned the airline's New York office. They were told that William Ellis had debarked at Kennedy International Airport. Had he boarded a plane for Bayport? No, he had not.

"Is his baggage in New York?" Joe asked.

After a long wait he got the answer. "No."

"Then perhaps it went through to Bayport."

"That's a possibility."

"Thanks for your help," Joe said, and he hung up.

"Let's find out right away," Frank said.

They jumped into their car and rode to Bayport Airport.

"If William's luggage has arrived," Joe said, "it might give us a clue."

The terminal was nearly deserted at that time of night, as most flights had already come in. The baggage master gave the boys his prompt attention. Several suitcases were still unclaimed. Could they possibly identify their friend's luggage?

It proved to be easy because one of the bags, a tan one that looked rather new, had William Ellis's name on it in bold white letters.

"That's it," Joe said. "May we take it?"

"Not without authority."

Joe went to a pay phone and called Chief Collig of the Bayport Police Department, a friend who had worked closely with them on many cases. He was not there, but the desk sergeant gave the boy his home phone number. When Collig answered, Joe outlined the case and said they were hoping to find a clue in William's bag.

"Like what?" asked the chief.

"I don't know. But can't we at least bring it to headquarters?"

The chief gave his permission and said that a patrol car would arrive shortly to pick up the suitcase.

When it arrived, the officer signed a receipt and drove to headquarters, with the Hardys following.

By the time they got there, Chief Collig himself had arrived. "This is interesting," he said. "I'd like to see what's in the bag."

The lock was picked by an expert and the suitcase laid open on the desk. In it were the usual things a young man would carry: slacks, a sport jacket, shirts, and a gift-wrapped package marked "Mrs. Hardy."

Chief Collig slit the paper and revealed a jar of preserves. "Looks like mangoes," he said.

"No doubt from William's mother," Frank said.

In a side pocket of the suitcase the chief found William's Swahili wordbook. A slip of paper marked a certain page and Frank opened it. On it were written two words: *Hatari Dingo.*

"*Hatari* means 'danger,'" Joe said and verified it in the book. But *Dingo* was not listed.

"Maybe it's one of those words that are seldom used," Frank said.

The contents of the suitcase were replaced and locked in the properties room for delivery to William if and when he should arrive.

The Hardys drove home. As they entered the driveway they saw a light in their father's second-floor study.

"Dad must be home," Frank said as he parked the car. "I wonder what's new in the ticket racket."

The boys hurried upstairs and found Fenton Hardy poring over a sheaf of notes.

"Dad, did you hear about William?" Joe asked.

"Mother and Gertrude told me," the detective replied. "A very serious matter. I'd say you'll have to relinquish the mask. It's not worth a human life!"

"What did you and Sam find out?" Frank asked.

"I think we have a good lead," his father replied. He told them that their investigation focused on a man named Kenleigh Scott, an employee of the printing plant who had been hired about six months previously.

"He's very bright," the detective went on, "and received several quick promotions. By his diligence he worked his way into the traffic department."

"So he knew the routes of all the trucks. Is that it?" Joe asked.

"Exactly."

"Did you question him?"

"I'm afraid not. He left without notice after the last big haul of tickets."

"What does he look like?" Frank wanted to know.

"The photos filed with Plant Security have disappeared," Mr. Hardy said, "but I'm confident that Sam can turn up something if he probes long enough. I left him on the case."

Now speculation turned back to the death mask, and Mr. Hardy had an idea. "Why don't you have a duplicate made at a foundry?" he suggested. "There's a good one in Millvale. A friend of mine, Alex Krusinsky, is a foreman. I'm sure he could take care of this with absolute secrecy. You might even try to palm the copy off on the crooks!"

"Terrific thought!" Frank said. "We'll see him first thing in the morning."

While they were still at the breakfast table the next day, Chet's jalopy bombarded its way down the street and their friend appeared at the back door, his freckled face beaming. "What do I smell, ham or sausage?"

"Sausage," Aunt Gertrude said. "Farm fresh."

"Can't say I'd turn it down," Chet remarked as he pulled up a chair. "And only two eggs, please, Aunt Gertrude. I've already had breakfast."

"We were just talking with Dad about *Bwana Brutus*," Joe said as he finished a glass of milk.

"Gives you the creeps, doesn't it, Mr. Hardy?" Chet shook his head. "A mysterious caravan that existed hundreds of years ago. I'm afraid its secret is buried in the sands of time."

"You're getting pretty poetic so early in the morning," Frank quipped. Then he added with a snap of his fingers, "You know, I just had a brainstorm."

"Let's hear it," Joe said.

"Suppose a cargo of gold disappeared on its way from Mali to Sijilmasa. And suppose it was hijacked and hidden. And suppose a smart man knew where it was and made a map."

"Go ahead," Fenton Hardy said. "It intrigues me."

Frank said that a parchment map could be destroyed, and so could wood. "That leaves metal, right?"

"Right!" Joe said. "The map might be on the death mask! Old *Bwana* Brutus might hold the key to the riddle!"

CHAPTER VIII

The Suave Stranger

"MAYBE the mask was the treasure in the captain's cabin, and was lost in the wreck of the *Africanus Rex*," Frank said.

"And I found it!" Joe was exuberant.

Chet put away his second fried egg and was savoring a sausage. "Fantastic!" he said. "And impossible!"

"Nothing is impossible, Chet," Mr. Hardy said. "Maybe Frank has something there."

"You know all the lines in those whiskers?" Frank went on. "They might camouflage the map that leads to the hiding place of the mysterious caravan!"

"It'll take time to work this out," Mr. Hardy said. "It might be a good idea to get a duplicate, even if you can't give it to the kidnappers."

"We'll go to the foundry right away," Joe said.

"Don't take it over yourself," Mr. Hardy advised. "Your enemies are desperate and might follow you. We'll have to do this by stealth."

They decided to call Tony Prito. He was to arrive in his father's truck, dressed in work clothes, and would bring a toolbox in which to carry the mask out of the house.

"That'll throw Stribling and company off the trail if they're spying on us," Joe said.

Tony agreed to cooperate. "Boy, just like a detective movie," he said. "I'll be there in half an hour."

When he walked into the kitchen, the boys got the mask from the safe and put it into the box Tony was carrying.

"I'll leave in our car a little later and meet you at the foundry," Joe said. "Frank wants to go to the library, in the meantime, to get some old maps of Africa."

Fifteen minutes after Tony had left, Joe drove to the foundry in Millvale, about ten miles away. He took a back road for a short cut. No one seemed to follow him. When he arrived, he looked for Tony's truck, but there was no sign of it.

"Good grief!" he thought. "I hope nothing has happened!"

Joe hurried into the foreman's office and asked Alex Krusinsky if the mask had been delivered.

"Not yet," the man replied. "Was it supposed to?"

Joe felt sick in the pit of his stomach. Had Tony been waylaid and the mask stolen? He told Krusinsky about his mission, looking out at the parking lot over and over again. Then he phoned Tony's home. Mr. Prito had not seen his son since he left the house with the truck.

Joe breathed deeply, trying to control his emotions. He made a second call to his father. Mr. Hardy answered and spoke in a low voice.

"I can hardly hear you, Dad," Joe said. He could sense his father putting his lips close to the mouthpiece.

"I can't talk any louder, Joe. A caller has just arrived, and I don't want to be overheard."

"Do you know what happened to Tony?" Joe asked, and he told his father about his futile search for the truck.

"No," Mr. Hardy replied. "But don't panic, Joe. Maybe the truck broke down. Just stay there till he comes and then hurry home. It's important."

"What is it, Dad?"

But Mr. Hardy had clicked off.

No sooner had Joe put the phone down, than he looked out the office window and saw Tony pull in. The boy parked and brought his toolbox inside.

"Where've you been, Tony?" Joe asked in an irritated tone. "You had me scared to death!"

"Flat tire! It does happen now and then, you know."

"Sorry. I didn't mean to snap at you," Joe said, and his friend opened the toolbox to remove the mask.

Alex Krusinsky looked it over carefully. "I can do a good job on this," he finally said. "Call me tomorrow."

"And don't forget," Joe warned, "it's strictly confidential."

"Don't worry. I'll do it myself."

The boys thanked him and left the office. On the way out Joe said, "Dad wants me to go right home for something important."

"Maybe word from the kidnappers?"

"He didn't say." Joe opened the door of his car. "Okay, chum, see you later. And thanks."

Both boys drove off, and Joe thought about his father's cryptic message all the way home. He pulled into the driveway, having noticed a convertible parked in front. A man was slouched behind the wheel, with only his peaked cap showing.

Joe entered through the kitchen door. As he went in, he could hear the conversation in the living room. The visitor had a mellifluous baritone voice that Joe could not identify.

The boy walked into the room and saw his parents and Aunt Gertrude having tea with a tall, handsome man. The suave, sun-tanned stranger was introduced to Joe as Elroy Abrams, a representative of the Jamaican Consulate. He rose to shake hands, then sat down again, crossed his legs comfortably, and looked Joe directly in the eye.

"I'll brief you quickly on my mission," he said. "Our government was alerted to the fact that you found an ancient mask on the beach in Jamaica. It is in the police report after the beating of Ali El Ansari. I have come to reclaim that mask. It belongs to the people of our country, you know."

"We were going to send it later, Mr. Abrams," Joe said lamely. Through his mind flashed the question: What if this man demanded the mask right now? And how would they satisfy the kidnappers? Should he tell the whole story to Abrams?

The man went on, "You should not have kept it at all!"

"We tried to return it before our flight home," Joe said. "But we ran into some trouble." He did not elaborate further. "Anyway, we got on the airplane with it. Just in time, too, I might say."

The man smiled ingratiatingly. "You won't be in any trouble if you turn it over to me now."

Joe perspired. "What a box I'm in!" he thought.

He was interrupted by the sound of Frank's

footsteps as he came through the front door and entered the living room. Frank was introduced to Abrams; then he looked nervously at his father.

"Dad, I must speak to you alone. Could you come upstairs for a minute? It's important."

Frank smiled at the caller. "You will excuse us, Mr. Abrams, but it's something that can't wait."

The man nodded amiably and addressed Laura Hardy, saying that she had two mighty fine sons.

When Frank and his father entered the study and closed the door behind them, the boy pulled a letter from his pocket. It was sent by air-mail, special delivery.

"I intercepted the postman on the sidewalk," Frank said. "It's from Sam Radley."

As Mr. Hardy slit it open, he said, "We're in a tight fix, Frank. That gentleman from the Jamaican Consulate wants us to turn over the mask pronto."

"Ye gods, and it's at the foundry!"

"Right. Maybe we can promise it for this evening. Trouble is, he is insistent and wants it immediately."

"Dad, we couldn't give it to him if we had it. What about William?"

Mr. Hardy had taken the letter from the envelope and a photograph fell to his desk.

"Oh, good," he said. "Sam got a picture of

our man Scott." He scanned the letter. "It was taken unknown to him at an employees' picnic," Radley had written.

Frank stared at the snapshot and gasped. "Oh, no!"

He took a magnifying glass from the desk drawer and focused on Scott. The people in the photo were magnified to twice their size.

The Hardys exchanged shocked glances. "No doubt, Dad," Frank said. "This man is in our living room *right now!*"

CHAPTER IX

The Clue in the Coat

THE suspense and excitement were nearly unbearable. Although the sound of their voices was well insulated from the floor below, Frank found himself talking in a whisper.

"Dad, what do you make of it? If the man is really the airline-ticket thief, why does he want the death mask? And how did he know about it?"

"Easy, Frank," his father replied. "Maybe there's a connection we don't know about, though he did show us his credentials. I'll phone the Jamaican Consulate in New York."

The operator gave Mr. Hardy the number, and his call went through in a few moments.

After the detective had identified himself, he said, "We have a visitor here named Elroy Abrams. He is representing himself as an official of the Jamaican Consulate. I'd like to verify his credentials."

A minute or two of silence followed. "No, Mr. Hardy," was the reply. "We have no person by that name in our employ."

"Then he must be an impostor!" Mr. Hardy said. After hanging up, he tapped out the number of Bayport Police Headquarters and spoke to Chief Collig, asking him to send two men over to arrest Abrams.

"Three squad cars are investigating an accident on the highway," the chief said. "But I'll have someone there as soon as I can."

"Well," Mr. Hardy said to Frank, "let's go down and see what Mr. Abrams-Scott has to say for himself."

"Are you going to nab him right away?"

"No. Not until the police arrive."

When father and son returned to the living room, Mrs. Hardy had just brought in another pot of tea and a tray of cookies.

"Good," Frank thought. "This'll give us the time we need."

The boy's heart was thumping at the bizarre situation. Joe seemed embarrassed to have the bogus official dun him for the mask. The women, in an affable mood, were chatting with the caller, whose charisma was undeniable.

After munching on a couple of cookies, for which he complimented his hostesses, the caller pressed his napkin to his lips and said with some finality, "Now what about the mask? I have to leave shortly to get back to New York. Joe, will you bring it to me?"

Joe was not often tongue-tied. In fact, Frank had never known his brother to lack for an answer. But this time Joe's mouth opened and no words came out.

Frank quickly took up the slack in the conversation. He had to keep the ball rolling until the police arrived.

"First of all," Frank said, "Joe and I want you to know that we appreciate your kindness. You've been fair with us, and we'll be fair with you, Mr. Scott."

Instantly the boy was stunned by his own blunder as well as by Scott's reaction, which hit like a thunderclap. Realizing he had been found out, the man overturned his tray, the utensils and china thudding onto the carpet. Joe was immobilized by the suddenness of it all. He thought the man had gone crazy!

Mrs. Hardy emitted a cry and Aunt Gertrude screamed, knocking over the half-empty teapot. The liquid spilled on Mr. Hardy's trousers. The impostor leaped up, grabbed his stylish leather coat, and tried to struggle into it while dashing for the door.

"Get him!" Mr. Hardy cried out. Frank lunged and so did Joe. The leather slipped through their fingers and Kenleigh Scott dashed down the front steps, still struggling to get into his coat.

Joe leaped from the top step, grasped the dangling sleeve, and hung on with bulldog tenacity. Scott whirled around. He struggled free of the garment and ran into the waiting car, the back door of which was open. Wheels skidded in the soft snow for a second; then the vehicle took off like a rocket.

Frank made a mental note of the license number. Then he groaned. "Where are the police? Why didn't they come in time?"

"Frank, will you tell me what this is all about?" Joe asked. "Why did Abrams flip his lid?"

"His name isn't Abrams," Frank said, as they returned, shivering, into the house. "That was Kenleigh Scott. We were just about to catch him when I blew it!"

Still shaking from the ordeal, Mrs. Hardy and her sister-in-law were busy cleaning up the mess on the living room floor. They were dazed by their guest's explosive departure, and when Mr. Hardy explained what had happened, Aunt Gertrude sank onto the sofa.

"A criminal! In our house!" she said weakly. "And we served him tea! Oh, dear, he might have murdered us all!"

Frank and Joe pitched in with the cleanup job until a squad car arrived. After the patrolmen were given a description of the getaway car, one of them immediately radioed headquarters. The other units would be on the lookout for it.

The impostor leaped up!

Shortly afterwards headquarters called back. It had been a rental car, signed out by an A. E. Dingo.

"Hey, Frank!" Joe exclaimed. "Dingo is the name in the Swahili wordbook! He's the one that William thought was dangerous!"

"Well, he got away this time," Frank said. He turned to his father. "I'm sorry, Dad. If we had caught Scott, you might have wound up your case quickly."

"Don't worry about it, son," Mr. Hardy replied. "It doesn't always work out that easily."

"Have you tried to figure out the double role of Kenleigh Scott in the ticket–mask mysteries?" asked Joe.

"That has me up a tree," the detective ruefully admitted. "But if there's an answer, we'll find it!"

Now the Hardy family was settled again after the frightening experience, and Mr. Hardy said, "Gertrude, don't wash these dishes."

"Goodness sakes! Why not? I'll use double-hot water on that cutthroat's cup!"

"Wait a minute. We need fingerprints," her brother replied. He assigned Frank to lift prints from the cup handle, the edge of the saucer, and the spoon. Then he examined the fine leather coat that now lay on the sofa.

"Look at the label, boys," he said. "It's from Paris."

"Expensive, no doubt," Joe said, as he felt the

material. "Kenleigh Scott must have lots of money from his ticket racket."

"I think it's kidskin," the detective went on, jotting down the name of the company. "We'll send them a cable asking for a list of possible dealers in the United States."

"I guess it's a long shot, Dad, but it's worth trying," Joe said.

Frank, meanwhile, had lifted two sets of prints from the cup and saucer. One was Aunt Gertrude's. The second, they felt sure, belonged to the impostor.

"Let's take them to Chief Collig," Joe suggested.

"How about sending a copy to Interpol?" Frank said. "If this airline-ticket racket is spread all over the world, Interpol might have something on our friend Scott."

"An excellent thought," Mr. Hardy agreed.

As they started to send the information out, Mrs. Hardy asked, "Fenton, where did Gertrude go?"

"She was here a minute ago. There she is, outside!"

"What is she looking at in the gutter?" Frank wondered.

Gertrude Hardy was bent down, tugging at something in the wet snow with her bare hands. The boys ran out to question her.

"Aunty, what's going on?" Joe asked.

"Humph!" she replied, straightening up. "You think you're the only ones who know how to look for clues?"

Joe winked at his brother and said, "Of course not. What have you got there?"

She held up what appeared to be a letter. It was soaked and crumbled from lying in the wet snow.

"This could have fallen from that scoundrel's pocket," Aunt Gertrude declared. "You spun him around like a pinwheel, Joe."

"All right, let's bring it inside to dry," Frank said. "And thanks for helping us."

Once indoors, Joe spread the soggy paper on the drainboard in the kitchen. The words, written in ink, were smudged and barely legible.

Aunt Gertrude went upstairs and returned minutes later with her hair dryer. She plugged it in and soon had warm air blowing on the mysterious letter.

"Maybe it's somebody's shopping list," Joe quipped.

"I wouldn't be too sure," Aunt Gertrude retorted tartly. "Fenton, come here and look at this! That's no shopping list at all!"

Mr. Hardy, who had been busy dispatching the information to Interpol and to the French company, came into the kitchen to examine his sister's find.

"There, it's showing up more clearly now," he

said. "Joe, we need a magnifying glass, the powerful one you keep in your desk."

Joe raced up the stairs, two at a time, and returned with the lens. He bent over to study the writing and his face grew beet red.

"It's—it *is* a clue, Aunt Gertrude!" he exclaimed.

"Then read it to us."

Joe sucked in his breath. "I can't make out all the words, only a few. They say, 'Get mask . . . us . . . and . . . will knock off Fenton Hardy.'"

CHAPTER X

A Muddy Race

"You know what this means?" Frank asked. "Dad's enemies and ours have gotten together somehow."

"You're right," Mr. Hardy said. "They're working together and are twice as strong now."

The boys felt sheepish when they complimented Aunt Gertrude on her good piece of detective work.

"We Hardys have to stick together," she replied with a coy smile. "I hope it helps you solve your case."

"Aunt Gertrude, you're something!" Joe said. "We're sorry we took it so lightly."

The next morning they called the foundry. "Is the job ready?" Joe asked.

"Yes. It turned out fine," Mr. Krusinsky replied. "Come and get it any time."

Another four inches of snow had fallen during the night, but since then the temperature had risen above freezing, and the roads were covered with a sloshy, slippery mess. With Frank at the wheel, they drove toward the foundry.

"I hope our scheme works," Joe said as they sped out into the open country. "We'll give up the duplicate mask for William and continue to study the original, if at all possible."

"Right," his brother said. "This investigation is a long way from being finished. Do you suppose we can catch the kidnappers?"

"It's going to be risky. But we're duty-bound to report it to the police."

"If we could only spring a trap and nail the whole gang!" Frank said.

They drove through farmland. Corn had been planted on both sides of the highway the summer before and the stubble poked through the fresh covering of snow. The boys had been watching the road behind them for possible spies, but it had been clear of traffic for several minutes. All at once, however, a red Ford sedan, traveling at high speed, pulled up close.

"I wish that guy would stop tailgating," Frank said. "If I had to brake suddenly, he'd climb right up my back!"

He drove as far to the right as he could to let the sedan pass. It did, but instead of streaking off, it slowed in front of them. When Frank tried to overtake the Ford, he was blocked!

"What's the matter with that joker?" Joe asked.

Just then another car appeared, as if from no-where, and positioned itself behind them. They were boxed in!

"We're in trouble, Joe," Frank said. "Did you get a look at these goons?"

The two men in the rear car wore ski masks pulled down over their faces, as did the driver in front. Their heads were covered except for eye slits and a mouth hole.

Frank tried again to pass the Ford, but it moved out to the center of the highway and their bump-ers banged. The Hardys were sandwiched in tighter than ever, and their tormentors brought them almost to a halt.

"They want us to stop," Joe said.

"Not on your life! I'm going to make a break for it!" Frank declared. They had come to a place where only a shallow ditch dropped off on the left side of the road. Frank watched for on-coming traffic. Now he had a chance!

Turning the wheel sharply and flooring the gas pedal, he broke out of the tight formation. Their right fender crumpled for a split second with a grinding crunch, but the car broke free!

Frank crossed the road, drove down into the ditch, and up the other side. "Look back, Joe. What are they doing?" he asked.

"Coming after us!"

"I think we can shake them off."

The soft snow on the muddy field in front of

them made driving treacherous. Frank drove in a tight semicircle, hoping to regain the highway and speed back to Bayport. Joe saw the trailing cars falling back.

"We've got it made!" he exulted.

Frank fantailed on the mucky topsoil and headed at full speed for the road. The rear wheels kicked up a rooster tail of snow and mud, and the motor growled as he urged every bit of horsepower from it.

But then—*slam!*

About a hundred yards from the side of the highway, the car stopped dead in its tracks.

"What happened?" Joe asked.

"Must have been a rock hidden by the snow," Frank said. "We're high centered!"

"Look, they're gaining on us!" Joe said. "The only thing left to do is to stand and fight."

The boys leaped from the car and got behind it while their pursuers raced up.

"If they hit the car, get ready to jump!" Frank told his brother.

The two other vehicles, however, slowed to a stop and the three men stepped onto the snow. They approached the Hardys, who stood poised for the attack. Besides being good boxers, they excelled in karate.

"We don't have the mask you're looking for!" Joe said hotly.

"We'll see for ourselves," one of the men replied. After searching the car in vain, their leader said, "We could drop you both in the snow right now, if we wanted to."

"Why don't you try?" Frank said.

"No. We don't want to hurt you. We want you to take a message back to your old man. Tell him to lay off his case! He's not dealing with a bunch of stumblebums this time!"

"So, what if he doesn't?" Joe demanded.

"That might just be the end of Fenton Hardy!" The men chuckled at the boys' predicament and drove away.

"Now what?" Joe asked.

"Here, put your shoulder to the back of the car."

The boys pushed and shoved, to no avail. The automobile was stuck tight.

"We'll have to go for help," Frank said. "There's a farmhouse on that ridge over there."

The brothers trudged across the field, past out-buildings and sheds, and knocked on the farmhouse door. A gray-haired man opened it. Frank introduced himself and his brother and said, "Can you help us, please? We're stuck in your field and can't get out."

"I saw them cars a while ago," the farmer said. "What was that, some fraternity initiation?"

"Nothing like that," Joe replied.

"Well, whatever it was, it was plumb crazy!"

"We're high-centered on a rock, sir," Joe said.

"I just ought to let you sit," the farmer grumbled. "Where'd this nonsense get you? Into trouble, that's where!"

"Perhaps we could use your tractor," Joe pleaded.

"It ain't working."

"Do you have a horse?"

"Yes. I got a horse. Two of 'em."

"Could we have them pull the car out?" Frank asked. "We'd be glad to pay you."

"I wouldn't take no money from no kids. Okay. I'll get the horses. But next time you're fooling around with your friends, don't play tag in my fields!"

The farmer put on boots and coat, and the Hardys followed him into the barn, redolent of hay and horses. The animals nickered and tossed their heads.

"Quiet! Easy there!" the man said.

Frank and Joe patted the horses while the farmer led them out of the barn. He harnessed the animals to a whiffletree and said to the boys, "You know how to handle horses?"

"Yes. We've done it before," Frank said.

"Okay. Take them and pull your car off the rock, then bring them back to the barn."

"You're very kind," Joe said. "Thanks for helping us."

The farmer replied with a grunt, and he went back into the house.

Frank and Joe walked the animals across the field, then hitched them to the front of the car.

Holding the reins, Frank said, "Giddap, there, fellows. Pull!"

The horses strained for a few seconds. With a scraping noise the underside of the chassis came free of the stone. Joe drove the car to the highway, while Frank took the horses back to the barn. After unharnessing them, he led them into their stalls. "Thanks, old boys."

When they arrived at the foundry, Krusinsky greeted them cordially. "Well, here you are," he said, showing them the two masks on his desk. "Can you tell 'em apart?"

"That's a great job!" Frank exclaimed. "I think you'd better tell us which is which."

The foundry man pointed to the original, then wrapped them up.

"How much do we owe you for this?" Joe asked.

Alex Krusinsky smiled. "Your dad said he'd take care of it later. Give him my regards. By the way, your mother has been trying to get you on the phone. She said you should have been here half an hour ago."

"Thanks," Frank said. "May I use your phone?"

"Sure. Go ahead."

Frank dialed the number and Mrs. Hardy answered. Her voice sounded nervous and she spoke fast. "Frank, they telephoned!"

"The kidnappers?"

"Yes. They left instructions. Hurry home as fast as you can!"

CHAPTER XI

Chet the Genius

GRABBING the package, the boys raced outside. Off they went toward Bayport, both looking grim and wondering what instructions the kidnappers had given.

They found Mrs. Hardy and Aunt Gertrude in the living room.

"What did they say, Mother?" Frank asked.

Mrs. Hardy picked up a piece of paper from an end table. "I made the notes right here," she said. "The kidnappers will meet you at two o'clock tomorrow morning."

"Where?"

"Behind Mary's Quick Stop."

"The little hamburger place on the Shore Road?" Joe asked.

"That's right. They have William, and they warned us not to notify the police."

"But we'll have to," Frank said.

"It's pretty woodsy out there," Joe added. "Good cover for a possible ambush."

Joe returned the masks to the Hardys' safe while Frank phoned police headquarters. Officer Kennedy answered.

"I don't know you, do I?" Frank asked.

The man replied that he had been on the force only three months. The desk lieutenant had been called away momentarily. What was it that Frank wanted?

"Is Chief Collig there?" Frank asked.

"No. Can I give him a message?"

"All right," Frank said, and he gave the rookie details of the kidnappers' phone call.

The boys paced about the house restlessly and only nibbled at their lunch. Mr. Hardy was out of town and would not return until later, so they could not consult with him.

"Listen, Joe," Frank said finally. "Let's work on the mask and compare the lines with the maps I got from the library."

The words were hardly out of his mouth when the telephone rang. It was Callie Shaw. "Iola and I can't get that spooky mask out of our minds," she said. "Can we help you any more?"

Joe chuckled. "You mean you want to come over?"

"Well——"

"Sure. We'd like to see you. Something's really brewing. We'll tell you when you get here."

The girls arrived in the Shaw family car, and when Frank told them about the kidnappers' plan their eyes danced with excitement.

"Oh, that'll be so dangerous!" Iola said. "You'll be careful, won't you?"

"Dad will be back by that time," Joe said. "Besides, the Bayport police probably will have the place staked out. When the crooks walk into the trap, *snap!* We've got 'em!"

"Joe's an optimist," Frank said, smiling. "It might not be all that easy."

After laying the work out on the dining-room table, Callie and Iola made rubbings of the mask, using the original. Then they inked in the lines of the face and beard.

"Among all these squiggles," Callie said, "might lie the secret."

"That's what we're hoping for," Frank said.

The four young people studied, compared, and repeated their efforts time and again. Finally Joe said, "I'm getting cross-eyed from all this." He sat back wearily, as his mother walked over.

"You need some fresh air," she said.

"Me, too," Frank muttered.

"Why don't you go ice-skating on Iola's pond for a while? You just can't sit around fidgeting until two o'clock in the morning."

The girls agreed and pulled Frank and Joe out of their seats. While Frank returned the mask to the safe, Joe gathered up the maps and tracings

and put them into a briefcase. "Let's take them
with us," he said. "Maybe we can work on them
later at your house, Iola."

"I'll chauffeur you," Callie offered. "You boys
can relax and rest your brains."

When they arrived at the Morton farm, Chet
was at the kitchen table, finishing a late lunch.

"I have some great news!" he said. "And some
bad news, too."

"Well, out with it!" Joe said.

"The good news is that school will be closed
for another two weeks at least. Just heard it on
the radio."

"How come?"

"The steam boiler broke down. It has to be
replaced and they can't get a new one right away."

"I would say that's bad news," Frank said.

"Oh, no. The bad news is that we'll have to
make up the lost time at the end of the year."

"That sounds logical," Callie commented.

"But it'll be almost summer by then," Chet
protested. "Sun shining, birds singing——"

Mrs. Morton interrupted Chet's reverie by asking if the young people wanted some hot choco-
late to fortify themselves. While they drank it,
they told Chet their latest news.

"Wow!" he exclaimed. "I hope everything goes
all right! You know, sometimes kidnappers kill
their victims!"

"Don't even think that," Frank said.

When they were finished, the young people took their skates and walked out behind the barn.

"You were right," Joe told Iola. "It's like a mirror."

While Callie and Iola donned their skates, the boys collected some firewood and soon had a bonfire burning on a knoll beside the pond.

"Now we won't freeze to death," Frank said as he put on his skates to join the others. They glided over the ice gracefully, doing figure eights and whizzing about the pond arm in arm. After a while they went to the fire to warm their cold hands and feet.

"I can't help thinking about William," Frank said. "Here we are, having a good time. I wonder what he's doing right now?"

"You'll have him back soon," Callie said kindly. "Worrying won't do you any good."

After half an hour of skating, Chet said, "Who's for snap the whip?"

The girls were given first chance at the end of the whip. Iola was to start. The whip snapped her at high speed, and she sailed around the edge of the pond, screaming in delight. Callie followed. She nearly lost her balance, but remained on her feet to enjoy the ride.

With rotund Chet anchoring the end of the line, Frank and Joe spun away like cannon shots, their friends cheering them on.

When it was Chet's turn, the five skated fast.

Then Frank anchored the line. Chet spun off at the end at terrific speed, and somehow lost his balance. His feet went out from under him and he landed on his back, his head hitting the hard ice.

Callie and Iola screamed and raced to the supine boy. Chet was stunned momentarily and did not move, and Frank put a hand under his shoulder to lift his head from the ice. At the same time Joe felt the back of Chet's head through the yellow skating cap.

"He's got quite a bump," Joe said. "Iola, will you bring a handful of snow?"

The girl skated to the edge of the pond and returned with the snow, which Joe applied to the contusion. Then they slid Chet carefully across the pond and carried him up gingerly beside the bonfire. There his sister rubbed more snow in his face and his eyes flickered open.

"Who—who turned out the light?"

"You got kayoed," Joe said.

"Ow!" Chet winced. He tested his muscles. Everything seemed all right with the exception of the bang on his head.

"I guess I'll survive," he decided. "But I've had enough skating. Let's go inside."

Mr. and Mrs. Morton had left to visit friends, having told Iola they would return later in the evening.

"I'm in charge now," Iola said, dimpling.

"Chet, you lie on the sofa until you feel better."

They decided not to tackle the riddle of the mask again until after supper.

Callie and Iola busied themselves in the kitchen, and even before the meal was ready, Chet walked in, sniffing the aroma.

"Out!" Iola demanded. "No picking! Dinner'll be ready in fifteen minutes."

The stuffed peppers the girls had made were eagerly devoured by the hungry skaters, and when the dishes had been cleared away, Frank spread the maps and tracings on the table.

"All right, let's start all over," he said. "Chet, you want to help?"

"I think you could use my expert assistance," the stout boy replied.

They worked for several minutes, overlaying the tracings onto the dozen or so ancient maps. Then Chet picked up one of the tracings. "Here, let me try."

"You've got it wrong-side up, dummy," his sister said with a chuckle.

"Hey! Wait! It matches!"

The young people looked dumbfounded at Chet's mistake.

"Good grief, he's right!" Frank said. "Would you believe it?"

"Chet, you're a genius," Callie exclaimed. "The fall on the ice must have done you some good!"

The boys reasoned that in order to make the riddle even more difficult to decipher, the person who made the mask had deliberately reversed the lines.

"See here?" Frank said, as he put the upside-down tracing on several more maps. "The lines correspond. All except one."

That one meandered up to the Atlas Mountains. "Today that would be southern Morocco," Iola said. "Where do you suppose the line stops?"

"Probably at the end of the route taken by the mysterious caravan," Joe guessed.

In high spirits the girls prepared duplicate copies on thin tissue for Frank and Joe, who folded them carefully and put them into secret compartments in their wallets.

"What about me?" Chet asked, hurt.

"The fewer of these around the better," Frank said. "Don't worry, Chet. We're giving you credit for the greatest discovery!"

"I want a dish of ice cream instead. All that brainwork made me hungry."

After another dessert for Chet, the friends parted, and Callie drove Frank and Joe home. Mr. Hardy was there when they arrived.

"Dad! We solved the riddle of the map!" Joe said, bursting into the house.

"Wait a minute," Frank said as he shucked his gloves. "You mean Chet solved it."

The three adults listened in amazement as the boys told their story.

"Well, what does all this mean?" Mrs. Hardy asked. "You're not going to Africa, are you?"

Frank and Joe looked at each other, and before they had a chance to reply, Aunt Gertrude spoke up.

"Laura, don't put such thoughts in their heads! Next thing you'll know they'll be off and we'll never see them again. Oh, dear! Pygmies and poisoned arrows, man-eating crocodiles, snakes——"

She clapped her hand to her forehead, and Mr. Hardy said, "Gertrude, please don't subject us to the horrors of your imagination!"

He turned to the boys. "Look, it's some time before two o'clock. I suggest we rest so we'll be fresh for the rendezvous."

"Dad, I want to check with the police again," Frank said.

"I've already done that," the detective replied. "Chief Collig has received the message from Officer Kennedy. The FBI was notified, too. All we have to do is to be at the designated spot with the duplicate mask at two o'clock."

Frank and Joe went to their room and lay down. Overstimulated, they lingered at the edge of sleep for an hour or so, never really dropping off to a deep slumber. They got up at one-thirty, after hearing their father on the floor below. Their mother and Aunt Gertrude were up to see them off.

Fenton Hardy drove the car, with the two boys seated beside him. Frank held the mask on his lap. The temperature had dipped below freezing again and the air was nippy, with stars shining brightly.

"Mary's Quick Stop is just around the next curve," Joe announced. The detective dimmed his lights and approached the place slowly. No one was in sight.

"I'll go around the back and we'll wait there," Fenton Hardy decided. A driveway circled the place; and once concealed near the rear entrance, their car could not be seen from the road.

The detective shut off the engine. They waited tensely. Joe switched on the radio and turned it very low. The dim beat of rock music was the only sound in the stillness.

Frank kept looking at his watch. Finally he said, "It's two o'clock exactly, Dad."

"They should be here any minute."

Just then a flashlight blinked at the side of the restaurant. The detective answered by turning his lights on and off quickly. As the three got out of the car, a voice said, "Put your hands up, all of you!"

The Hardys did, Frank holding the mask high above his head.

Now the speaker appeared. He wore a ski jacket and a mask. Behind him stood the tall figure of William Ellis.

"You're covered, so don't make a false move!" the criminal said. "Give me that mask!"

Frank stepped forward and turned it over. To himself he thought frantically, "Where are the police? When is the trap going to be sprung? Now is the time!"

In the dim starlight the boy tried to make out the face behind the mask. But there was no chance of recognition.

Now the Hardys noticed that William was blindfolded, with his hands tied behind his back. The man shoved him in the back, and he stumbled into Frank's arms.

"He's all yours," the kidnapper grumbled, and William gave a small sigh of relief.

"Don't worry, William," Joe said. "You're safe now."

As the kidnapper retreated along the side of the restaurant and out of sight, Joe said, "Dad, what happened to the police? They should have been here!"

"Somebody must have goofed," his father replied. Seconds later a motor sounded, and with its lights switched off, the car drove away from Mary's Quick Stop.

"They're taking off!" Frank shouted and ran to the front.

CHAPTER XII

Sign of the Ju-Ju Man

MR. HARDY waited a few more minutes, then turned on the engine, and was just about to drive away when three sets of headlights zipped down the road. Approaching Mary's Quick Stop, the lights were turned off and the cars proceeded more slowly.

"Jumping Catfish!" Joe declared. "It's the police!"

The silhouette of their domes became visible as the squad cars blocked the Hardys' exit. A number of men jumped out with flashlights illuminating the detective and the boys.

"What happened to you?" Mr. Hardy demanded as he stepped out of his car.

Chief Collig, who was in the lead, looked embarrassed. "We thought it was Tom and Mary's Diner down the road about a half mile."

"Oh, nuts," Frank said in disgust. "I wondered whether Kennedy got the message fouled up."

"He's new on the force." Collig tried to apologize. He turned to the other men, including three agents from the FBI and told them that obviously a mistake had been made in the location.

"Well, the kidnappers are gone now," Mr. Hardy said. "That way." He pointed. "We have the hostage, safe and sound. He'll be available for questioning later."

"Fine. We'll get a statement from him tomorrow," Chief Collig said, and the police took off in the direction of the kidnap car.

On the way back to Bayport, the grateful William described his ordeal. When he had reached New York, two men who claimed to be operatives for Mr. Hardy duped him into thinking that Frank and Joe were waiting in the city.

"They did not look at all like criminals," the boy said.

"Not all of them do," Mr. Hardy said. "Then what happened?"

William described how they had entered a small hotel, where he had been seized, bound, and gagged. "They pushed me into a closet near the reception desk. After about an hour, I was taken into a car and driven a long way to what seemed like the country. A quiet place, with not much traffic."

"They probably hid you near Bayport," Mr. Hardy surmised. "Did you overhear anything?"

"They talked about the mask. The reason why they want it so badly is that according to a legend they heard, the clue to the treasure on the *Africanus Rex* was on a mask. It seems that it was the secret hidden in the captain's cabin."

"Right!" Joe said. "We arrived at the same conclusion!"

"They forced Ali to tell them about the inscriptions," William went on. "Then they tried to figure out what they meant, but could not."

"We did!" Joe said. He explained how the lines on the beard actually traced the route of the ancient Sahara caravans.

"That was very clever!" William said in admiration.

"Wouldn't it be great to go treasure hunting in Africa?" asked Joe as they approached Elm Street.

"You know, that's a super idea," Frank said. "We could take William with us. His knowledge of Swahili might come in handy!"

"You must be jesting," the Jamaican said. "Aren't they, Mr. Hardy?"

"Stranger things have happened," the detective replied. "We'll talk more about it later."

Mrs. Hardy and Aunt Gertrude were still up when they arrived, and the women were delighted to see that William had been released unhurt.

"You must be starving," Mrs. Hardy said. "I'll make you a sandwich. Would you like it toasted?"

"Yes, ma'am, please."

All the while Gertrude Hardy studied their midnight guest. As he ate, she adjusted her spectacles, peered over them, then concentrated her gaze through the lenses.

Joe nudged her and whispered, "Don't stare at him like that, Aunty."

"He's a handsome boy," his aunt replied, "and so polite."

"Then you won't mind if he goes to Africa with us?"

Aunt Gertrude smiled benignly. "That's out of the question. School is going to be in session."

"But it's closed. Haven't you heard? The boiler broke down."

"Good heavens! That would be the end of all of you, traipsing around in Africa!"

When William had finished eating, Mr. Hardy said, "We'd better turn in now. William can talk to the police in the morning and pick up his bag."

"Oh, you have it?" the boy asked.

"It's at headquarters."

"Good. There is something very special in it."

"What?" Joe pried.

"You will see tomorrow."

William was shown to the guest room, and soon

the Hardy home was quiet. Later that morning everyone was jarred awake by the ring of the telephone. Chet and Iola were on the line, asking about William.

"He arrived safely," Frank said. "But the crooks got away." He briefly sketched what had happened, then said, "We've got a lot to do this morning, Chet. See you later."

After breakfast the boys took their guest to headquarters. Chief Collig was there to meet them. He apologized for the fiasco, then took a long statement from William about his experience with the kidnappers.

"And now may I have my suitcase?" the boy asked.

"We took the liberty of looking through it for clues," Frank said. "I hope you don't mind."

"Not at all. Did you happen to read my note on Dingo?"

"Sure did," Joe said, and he told William how Dingo had driven the phony Jamaican envoy in his escape from the Hardy home.

"And the preserves?" William went on. "You did not open them, did you?"

"No. Of course not."

They drove off with the luggage and as soon as they entered the Hardy home, William gave the jar to Mrs. Hardy. "It is from my mother," he said, "but there is something in it for Frank and Joe."

While the others looked on, Mrs. Hardy un-
screwed the cap. Inside were delicious stewed
mangoes. She poured them into a serving tureen,
and as she did so, an aluminum tube, about three
inches long, fell out with the fruit.

"What's this?" Mrs. Hardy said, removing it
with a spoon.

William wiped the tube and took off the metal
cap. An unusual piece of ivory on a chain fell out.

"A lion's tooth," the Jamaican explained,
holding it up for the others to see. "Inlaid with
copper. It is the sign, or signature, of a *ju-ju* man.
I hid it in the mangoes for safekeeping."

William said that the ancient relic had come
from Ghana and was the gift of Ali El Ansari.
"He took quite a liking to Frank and Joe."

"What's a *ju-ju* man?" Joe asked.

"He is like a medicine man to the American
Indians," William said. "According to the natives,
the *ju-ju* man has magical powers. If one puts a
curse on you, it will take another, more powerful,
ju-ju man to remove it."

"I'd like to put a curse on those crooks!" Joe
said with a wry smile.

Frank took the lion's tooth from William and
examined it closely. "This is beautiful inlay
work," he said.

"You wear it, Frank," William said and he
placed the relic around the boy's neck.

The rest of the morning Frank and Joe drove

William around Bayport, but not before he was warmly dressed in one of Joe's sweaters and Frank's ski jacket, which fit him snugly. A pair of Mr. Hardy's gloves completed the outfit.

Halfway through the sightseeing tour, the boy said, "Man, I am cold. You know, I have never seen winter before!"

"What about snow?" Joe asked.

"First time, too."

"You wouldn't object to a little snowball fight to warm up, would you?" Frank asked. He stopped along the side of the road, where a snow plow had formed a mound.

When the boys got out, the Hardys showed William how to make snowballs. After preparing an arsenal of six apiece, they fired.

"Hey, he's got quite an arm," Frank said, as he ducked a flying snowball. William's next shot knocked Joe's hat off, and he laughed gleefully.

"Look who's coming!" Frank said suddenly.

With a triple bang, Chet parked his jalopy behind the Hardys' car. The stout boy jumped out, tilting his yellow cap down over his eyes. After greeting William, he said, "Listen, this is no time for a snowball fight. I just came from your house. Good thing I found you."

"What happened?" Joe asked.

"Plenty," Chet said with an air of authority. "Cablegrams, suspects, plans for Africa." He beamed. "And I think I'm going with you!"

"Oh yes? Don't be too sure," Joe said. "They have enough elephants there already."

Chet looked insulted. They got into their cars and he followed the trio back to Elm Street. Mr. and Mrs. Hardy were eating lunch, but Frank knew something exceptional must have happened. His father's cool demeanor was seldom ruffled by either good news or bad, but now he seemed excited.

"Tell us what's going on, Dad!" Frank urged, as the boys joined their parents at the table.

"Your case and mine seem to be breaking fast," the detective stated. "I just got a cable from the company in Paris. That leather coat Kenleigh Scott left behind him was custom made at an Arabian shop in the *souq* of Marrakesh."

"In the what?" asked Chet, wrinkling his freckled nose. "What's a *souq*?"

"A marketplace," William told him. "All kinds of things are sold there."

"Then Scott must be an Arab," Joe said.

"Not necessarily," Mr. Hardy said. "Custom-made leather goods are produced in Morocco for customers all over the world. But listen to this. I've just been informed that an airline-ticket-theft suspect named Jason Hickson was nearly caught by police in New York. He eluded them, and later it was learned that he had taken a plane to Casablanca."

"And was caught there?" Frank asked.

"No. He got away again," Mr. Hardy replied. He pulled a picture from his pocket. "See, that's the fellow." Hickson was a short man with a broad, pudgy face and a thin mustache on his upper lip.

"Two good clues. And I know what you're going to say," Frank said.

"Right," Joe added. "There's a Morocco connection!"

"Exactly. Your idea of going to Africa might not be a bad one," Mr. Hardy said. "In fact, you have the assignment if you'd like it."

"You mean it?" Frank asked. He grinned broadly.

"Yes. Three different airlines have agreed to defray expenses. They'll pay for two detectives and two assistants."

Chet let out a startling yell. "That means I can go! Boy, I'll be the greatest assistant!"

Mr. Hardy turned to William. "How would you like to join my sons?"

"That would be my distinct pleasure," William replied, excitement shining in his dark eyes.

Before Frank and Joe had a chance to discuss anything with Chet, they heard the door close, Chet's engine start, and his jalopy pull away.

"Wow!" Joe laughed. "He's off like Paul Revere!"

For the rest of the day the Hardy home was busy with phone calls, one of them to Marrakesh, where the detective had a friend, Dr. Henri Cellier. Mr. Hardy explained that he had met the doctor, who was now head of the Avenzoar Hospital, in New York years before.

"Henri was a medical student when I was a rookie in the New York Police Department," Mr. Hardy said. "He's a grand fellow, and we became good friends."

When the call to Marrakesh went through, Fenton Hardy renewed his old acquaintance and told Dr. Cellier that his sons, with their two friends, would arrive in a day or two. Would he give them a hand in their work? Dr. Cellier said he would do everything in his power to assist the boys and that he would get in touch with them on their arrival in Casablanca.

While all the preparations were underway, Mrs. Hardy and her sister-in-law looked on quietly. It was obvious that they were apprehensive, thinking of the safety of the four boys in a strange continent.

"Please don't worry about us," Frank said. "We've got William to help us, and Chet, who's proven his reliability many times. As a matter of fact——"

Mrs. Hardy, who was looking out the window, suddenly shrieked, her shoulders shaking.

"Mother!" Frank exclaimed. "Are you laughing or crying?"

"L-look!"

Somebody clomped onto the porch and Joe opened the door. There stood Chet Morton! He wore tan shorts, a military blouse with epaulets, and a pith helmet. A canteen was slung over his shoulder.

"Hey, let me in quick!" he cried out. "I'm freezing!"

CHAPTER XIII

The Spooky Villa

"CHET, you'll catch pneumonia and won't be able to go to Africa with us!" Joe said.

"Don't worry, I'll warm up in no time." Chet danced a jig, which looked even more comical because of his red legs and short pants.

The fun over, the boys settled down to the serious business of making plans. William called his parents, who gave him their permission to take the trip. Then a travel agent booked them from Bayport to Kennedy International Airport in New York and on to Casablanca, where they got reservations at the Hotel Marhaba.

"When you get there, telephone the United States Consul, John Klem, and make an appointment to see him," Mr. Hardy suggested. "He'll brief you on Morocco, and you'll be oriented in no time at all. Also, read up on the country in the encyclopedia."

The boys spent the entire evening doing that. Morocco, they learned, was once under French control, and the French language was still widely spoken along with Arabic. One-hundred-thousand Frenchmen were scattered about the country. Arab women wore caftans and the men, djella-bahs. But the ordinary street dress was the bur-noose, a long, hooded cloak.

Early the next morning the Hardys dispatched Chet to pick up their tickets at the travel office, and after lunch they started out for the airport. After Phil, Tony, and Biff had given their friends a surprise send-off, the four boys caught the plane to New York and did not have to wait long for the connecting flight. The ride over the Atlantic was pleasant, and when they touched down in Casablanca, the companions took a taxi directly to their hotel. They were assigned two adjoining rooms on the sixth floor.

Frank phoned Mr. Klem immediately. The consul's secretary said he was out for the day and set up an appointment for the following morning.

"Thank you," Frank said. "By the way, can you recommend a good restaurant? We'd like to try the native food."

"There's no finer dining place than Al Mounia," she replied. "It's really beautiful, and the *cous-cous* is out of this world."

"What's that?"

"Order and you'll see," she answered, laughing. "But easy with the sauce. It's very hot."

The friends spent the day driving around the city. The hotel concierge suggested that they rent a *carrossa,* a horse-drawn carriage, so as to take in the sights leisurely.

All the main streets radiated from a hub in the center. Like spokes on a giant wheel, the thoroughfares went in every direction of the compass and were lined with gleaming white buildings.

The boys stopped their driver and browsed through curio shops, where William was particularly interested in art objects made by the black tribes south of the Sahara desert.

"Look at this!" he said. "The kind of dog I always wanted." In his hands he held a carving of a small, lightly built animal with a short back, which seemed to be set high on the legs compared to its length. It had a wrinkled forehead and carried its head proudly. The dog's demeanor was poised but alert.

"What breed is it?" Chet asked.

"It's a Basenji," William replied, "an African dog. Look at that sleek head!"

"I've heard about them," Frank said. "But I've never seen one."

William had, in Jamaica, and vowed that some day he would have one. "As far back as three thousand B.C.," he said, "these dogs were favorites of the pharaohs in Egypt. They disappeared from sight for centuries, and finally were rediscovered as companions of the pygmies in the African Rain Forest."

"Basenji sounds like a Swahili word," Joe said.

"It is, and it means a 'wild thing,' " William explained. He added with a grin, "This dog's bite is worse than his bark, because the Basenji does not bark at all. He makes a noise almost like a chortle or a yodel."

Joe took the carving and handed it to the clerk. "William, you now own your favorite breed. It's a gift from us to you."

The dog was wrapped, paid for, and presented to the Jamaican boy, who thanked the Hardys warmly.

Then Chet said, "Listen, fellows. It's getting near that time."

"Okay, Chet," Frank said. "Are you all set to try the *cous-cous?*"

"I would try *cous-cous*, goose-goose, or moose-moose," Chet said, patting his belt. "Sightseeing makes me hungry."

Their driver dropped them off at Al Mounia and Frank told him not to wait. Then they entered a walkway leading to the restaurant, with its Moorish arched façade.

"Those mosaics are beautiful," William said. "It looks more like a museum than an eating place."

The inside was even more impressive. The

walls and ceilings were also covered with colorful mosaics. Instead of sitting at tables, diners sat on divans around the walls.

The maitre d'hotel, in formal clothes, ushered the boys to one of them, and they sat down on the low cushioned seats. A colorfully dressed black man presented them with large menus. He wore a white jacket, red fez, white stockings, and black pantaloons.

"Hey, this is really cool!" Chet said. "Nothing like Bayport."

The boys ordered and waited expectantly. It did not take long for the waiter to bring a large silver tray laden with food. First, he spooned out a pile of *semolina* on each plate.

"Looks like rice," Joe commented.

Around it, the man carefully arranged raisins, onions, carrots, chick peas, and turnips. Over this he ladled chunks of lamb and yellow broth, which was quickly absorbed by the *semolina*.

Beside each plate he placed a small dish of condiment. The sauce, he indicated, was to be put on the meat.

"Well, here we go," said Chet. He had been gazing around at other diners, paying no attention to what the waiter said. "I think I'll try a little of the soup first."

Eagerly he put a spoon into the sauce and before the Hardys could stop him, swallowed a mouthful. Immediately he had spasms of choking. His face grew red, and he reached for a glass of water. Chet drank it down, his eyes rolling and sweat pouring from his forehead. His voice was a hoarse whisper as he slid off the divan. "I-I've been poisoned."

"No you haven't," Joe said as the waiter rushed up with another glass of water.

"That's not soup," Frank said. "It's a condiment. A little bit goes a long way!"

He helped Chet to his seat, and the boys began to eat their meal eagerly.

About halfway through, the waiter moved unobtrusively to Frank's side and pressed a note into his hand.

The boy read the message. "It's from Mr. Klem," he told the others. "He wants to see us immediately." The note gave the consul's home address.

"We're not going to fall for that one, are we, Frank?" Joe asked.

"You mean it might be a trap?" William said.

"It's probably phony," Joe said, and Frank was inclined to agree. He signaled the manager, who hastened over to them.

"*Oui, Monsieur,*" he said. "Is everything satisfactory?"

"The food is wonderful," Frank replied. "By the way, do you know Mr. Klem, the United States Consul?"

"*Oui.* Very well. Is he a friend of yours?"

"We've never met him," Frank said. "But I just received a message asking us to his home."

"I-I've been poisoned!" Chet rasped.

"Who gave it to you?"

Frank pointed to the pantalooned waiter, who had overheard the conversation and quickly explained that the note had been given to him by a taxi driver.

"The address is authentic," the maitre d'hotel said, glancing at the note. "If there is any doubt, why don't you telephone *Monsieur* Klem?"

"That's a good idea," Frank said. He was directed to a phone near the entrance. He dialed the number and received a busy signal.

He returned to the table and told his friends about the call. "At least someone's home," he said. "Shall we go?"

"I think so," Joe decided. "Maybe Klem's secretary told him that we were here. And obviously he is known at Al Mounia."

"Hey, fellows," Chet said, "I don't feel so hot. Maybe that sauce did me in."

"Tell you what," Frank said. "You and William go back to the hotel, while Joe and I visit Klem. Okay?"

Chet nodded, and the boys paid their bill. On the way out Frank tried the consul's number again. It was still busy.

As they stepped into the street, a taxi pulled up to the curb in front of them. The driver, a smiling Arab wearing a burnoose, jumped out and opened the door.

"You go ahead," Chet said to the Hardys. "We'll get another cab."

"Right. See you later."

The Hardys climbed in and showed the driver Klem's address. After ten minutes, Frank said, "I thought he'd live in a nice residential area. Look, Joe, this seems more like a slum!"

The road finally ran into a sparsely settled part of town, and the man stopped in front of a low, white villa that sat far back from the street. A dim light was shining inside.

"You're sure this is the right address?" Frank asked the driver as he paid him.

"Oui, Monsieur."

"You stay here," Joe added, "so you can take us back to our hotel."

But as soon as the boys walked toward the house, the driver quickly started off.

"How do you like that?" Frank said. "You suppose he doesn't understand English?"

"I don't like this at all," Joe commented as they cautiously approached the front door. "It's spooky here." He noticed another car coming out of the darkness in the distance.

Frank pressed a bell. The door flew open and a bright light flashed into their faces. Four strong hands reached out and grabbed the boys!

Frank and Joe struggled to escape as the car stopped in front!

CHAPTER XIV

Foiled by a Donkey

FRANK and Joe fought furiously to keep from being dragged into the house. Then two figures jumped from the car and raced up the walk.

Chet and William!

Without a word, they pitched into the fray and pulled the Hardys loose.

"Let's get out of here quick!" Chet panted. They ran to the waiting taxi and sped off. There was no pursuit.

"Take us to the police," Frank told the driver. He turned to Chet. "How come you arrived just in the nick of time?"

"Well, we felt we were copping out on you," Chet explained. "We didn't know whether it was a trap or not, so we decided to follow—a backup team, so to speak."

"Good thing you did," Joe said wryly. "How's your stomach?"

"In all that excitement I forgot about it."

When they arrived at headquarters, the Hardys took turns explaining what had happened to them. But the officer at the desk shrugged, his arms outstretched. "I do not speak the English so good," he said.

The boys tried to use their high school French, but with no better results. The officer seemed as baffled as they were. On the way back to their hotel, Joe said, "What a way to start an investigation in Africa. Our cover's blown already!"

"We have probably been spied on ever since we landed," William surmised.

"It gives me a creepy feeling," Chet said. "Now it's getting real dangerous."

"But who are they?" Frank thought aloud. "The goons from the ticket racket or the treasure hunters?"

"Who knows?" Joe said. "Maybe both."

After breakfast the next morning the young sleuths went directly to the office of the United States Consul. Mr. Klem, a short, slender, balding man, greeted them cordially and listened attentively to their story.

Finally he said, "About your father's case—the airline-ticket racket—we've had trouble here, too. The police have no leads, and I know anything you can do to help them would be appreciated."

Frank said, "And have you heard about an ancient mysterious caravan?"

The official explained that many legends and rumors abounded about ancient treasure in the Atlas Mountains, but he could tell them nothing substantial. "Perhaps you can learn more when you go to Marrakesh," he concluded.

Just then the phone on his desk rang. He listened for a moment and looked up at his visitors. "There's a caller for you," he said.

The door opened, and the boys turned to see a beautiful dark-haired girl enter. She seemed to be about eighteen years old, slim and lithe. Her slightly almond-shaped eyes flashed over the Americans and she smiled. "Frank and Joe Hardy?" she asked in a lilting French accent.

"That's us," Joe said. "Over there's Frank."

"Then this must be Chet Morton and William Ellis. Am I right? Mr. Klem and I have met before."

The man rose from behind his desk and said, "Mademoiselle Christine Cellier."

"Dr. Cellier's daughter?" Frank asked.

"Yes," she said. "Father sent me to help and I found out from the concierge at your hotel that you would be here."

"That's great," said Chet. "We could use a guide."

Christine said that she would spend the day with the boys and would then accompany them to Marrakesh to meet her family the following morning. "I am staying overnight with an aunt here in Casablanca," she explained.

The young Americans thanked the consul and left with their new friend. They walked along the street until they came to a sidewalk cafe.

"Let's stop here and sit down," Frank said.

Over frosty glasses of coke, the young people relaxed and talked. Christine laughed when she heard about the *cous-cous*. This led to discussion of the frightening experience of the evening before; then Frank told the girl about their father's case.

"I think a travel agency might be a good cover for such a ticket-theft gang," he concluded. "Maybe we should check out all such places in Casablanca."

"I will be glad to help you," Christine said. "There is one that I know well, and others we can go to."

When they had finished, the five visited the three largest agencies in town. The people were very cordial and said that as far as they knew, the ticket racket had made little progress in their city.

In the *Agentur d'Este,* where Christine knew the proprietor, the Hardys picked up their first clue. The owner said that a new agency had opened in a very old part of town, which was odd. It was not known to tourists, and was rarely frequented by business people. The man shook his head. "Where they get their trade, I do not know."

"You think it is worth investigating, Frank?" William asked.

"Definitely. Let's go."

They stopped long enough for a snack before the girl led them into a run-down part of town, located some distance from the commercial center. The narrow streets were cobblestoned, and very old houses were built against one another. The doors, flush on the sidewalk, opened into dark interiors.

Finally Christine said, "Here is the place."

It was no more than a hole in the wall with a sign over the door in Arabic. "World Travel Agency," Christine translated.

The office was so small that there was room only for Frank, Joe, and the girl. The other two remained outside.

A man appeared from the back room, noticed the three, and quickly ducked out of sight again. The Hardys pretended not to see. But Joe moved Frank aside and whispered, "That fellow looked familiar!"

"He's the cabbie who set us up last night!" Frank said.

The man, who now wore European dress instead of the burnoose, did not come back. Christine called out in French, then in Arabic. Finally the three stepped out again into the blazing sunlight.

Quickly they told Chet and William about the suspect. "Let's split up and stake this place out," Frank suggested. "Joe, you and William see if there's a back door. The rest of us will watch the front."

"Roger."

Joe and the Jamaican hurried down the street, turned into a side lane, and went around behind the travel agency.

"This should be it," Joe said. They concealed themselves in a doorway and watched. Within a few moments, the suspect poked his head out and looked around cautiously, but did not see the boys. Then he closed the door behind him, locked it, and turned left, down an alley. It grew so narrow that it was possible to leap over the rooftops from one side to the other.

Joe and William followed him, bumping into Arabs in their haste. Then they heard the cry "*Balik! Balik!*" A bearded man approached, leading a donkey. The beast's back was piled high with rugs, which nearly touched the buildings on each side of the alley.

The boys tried to squeeze past the load, but could not. They had to press themselves tightly against a building as the cargo passed.

"I guess we learned an Arabic word," Joe said. "It must mean 'out of the way!' "

William nodded. "So is our man. I cannot see him any more."

"He disappeared!" Joe said grimly. "Let's go

back to the others before we lose them, too."

They found Frank, Chet, and Christine still staking out the front entrance of the travel agency, and explained how the suspect had slipped away.

"Nothing happened on this end," Frank reported, "except that the guy locked the front door."

"He did the same at the back entrance," Joe said.

"Well, we know for sure there's something fishy going on," Chet said.

"This could be a branch of the ticket thieves," Frank agreed. "But now that they're tipped off, it will be hard to find evidence."

They walked back to the center of town, and looked at exotic merchandise displayed by vendors, whose little shops extended nearly to the curb. Several colorful hassocks made of multicolored goatskin intrigued Frank and Joe.

"Let's send one home," Frank suggested.

Christine helped them pick out an unusual design of red and black and bargained with the shopkeeper over the price.

"*La,*" she kept saying. "*La.*"

The merchant gestured with a pleading expression until Christine finally agreed that the price was fair enough.

"Something you should remember in Morocco," she said, smiling. "You have to bargain, otherwise you pay double the price and the merchant is insulted. *La* means 'no.' "

"I figured that," Joe said.

"Now you have a nice pouf," she added, and made arrangements to have it shipped to Bayport.

"I'd like to buy a dagger," Chet said.

"Not here," Christine objected. "Wait till you see the *souq* in Marrakesh. They make beautiful ones there."

"They also make clothing out of leather, don't they?" Frank said.

"Yes. That's a specialty."

The boys returned to their hotel, where Christine said, "I would like to introduce you to Father."

"Is he here?" Chet asked.

"No. In Marrakesh. But I promised to call him."

They phoned the Moroccan city, which lay many miles inland on a hot desert plain. When Dr. Cellier answered, Christine introduced the boys.

"Ah, Frank, I have a cable from your father," the doctor told him. "It came this morning." He read it carefully. "Interpol identified fingerprints. Scott international thief. Born Frenchman. Speaks many languages, including Arabic."

Frank relayed their experience in Casablanca and the doctor said, "I do not like this. Your enemies must have been shadowing you. I suggest you check out of your hotel and try to evade them."

Frank thanked him, hung up, and told the others about his conversation.

"If Scott speaks Arabic," William reasoned, "he could be operating here in Morocco."

"Or, for that matter, anywhere in North Africa," Christine added.

Frank was thoughtful. "Your father is right," he said. "Our enemies can strike any time. They know where we are. Let's leave this place and get rooms somewhere else."

"It is past check-out time for the day," William noted.

"We won't check out. We'll just leave quietly and let the concierge think we're still in our rooms."

Christine knew of a small hotel nearby, on the way to the railroad station where they would take the train next morning. One at a time, the boys unobtrusively carried their luggage out through a back entrance and followed Christine. They took a large room with two double beds.

"I am going to visit my aunt now," Christine said when they were checked in. "I will see you tomorrow morning at ten."

After supper, the boys watched television in the lobby. A French film was showing. Eventually they got bored since they could not follow the foreign language.

"Let's get some sleep," Frank said. They went to their room, which looked out over the city.

"We can see the Marhaba from here," Chet noted. "Matter of fact, even the windows of our rooms."

As they skinned into their pajamas, the night sounds were interrupted by the strident hee-haw of sirens.

"Boy, that's a funny sound," Chet said. "Is it fire engines?"

William looked out the window and called to the others. "Look at the Marhaba!"

The side of the hotel was illuminated by floodlights.

"Good night!" Frank exclaimed. "Smoke's coming out of our windows!"

CHAPTER XV

The Spy at the Wall

A phone call to the Marhaba Hotel revealed that the rooms occupied by the boys had been fire-bombed.

"Two men broke into your quarters," said the concierge. "We are very sorry. If your baggage was destroyed, we have insurance——"

"Don't worry about it," Frank said. "We won't be back."

"Frank, I am glad we followed Dr. Cellier's advice," William said. "We might have been killed had we stayed there!"

"Which proves," said Joe, "that we've come very close to the operation of the ticket thieves."

"Too close for comfort," Chet added as he watched the smoke from the windows dissipate and the spotlights finally wink off.

The boys decided to return to World Travel the next morning. "If someone's there," Frank said, "we might get a line on what's doing."

After an early breakfast, they set off toward the back alleys. Proceeding carefully through the labyrinth, they arrived at the office.

A sign in Arabic was posted against the door, which was locked. "This probably says 'closed,' " William said.

Joe noticed a woman dressed in a caftan, standing across the street. Her eyes, peering over the black veil followed their every move. Crouched directly above the boys on the rooftops was a man in a white burnoose. The woman sent him a hand signal.

"Let's get out of here before we're attacked!" Chet urged.

Frank agreed, and the boys retreated casually. At the hotel, Christine met them promptly at ten, bright faced with enthusiasm. When they told her what had happened, her eyes opened wide.

"I think it is best to leave Casablanca right away," she said. "At least in Marrakesh there will be some protection. My father is an influential man. By the way, I made reservations at the Hotel Manzur for you."

The boys thanked her, and they went to the railroad station. They boarded the train, took seats, and were soon rumbling eastward over the desert.

"There will not be much to see until we reach

our destination," Christine said, looking out over the barren landscape. Sand, a few palm trees, camels, goats, and scrubby farms, no larger than an acre or two, flashed by.

After a couple of hours a vendor arrived, selling sandwiches and drinks.

"I thought you'd never come," Chet said. He bought something for everybody.

Christine put her head close to Frank's and said, "See the man in the djellabah over there, on the other side?"

The boy slowly moved his eyes in that direction. "The Arab eating the sandwich?" he asked.

"Yes. Watch what he is doing with his right hand."

At first the boy saw nothing unusual, but then he noticed that the man was rolling a piece of bread into a tiny ball.

Christine leaned close again. "He is not an Arab, Frank. He is a Frenchman. That is an idiosyncracy of the French, especially of the people who live in the Gueliz, the French quarter of Marrakesh."

"Another spy?" Frank asked.

"Possibly."

When the fellow disappeared from his seat for a minute or two, Frank told the others, and they kept an eye on the man until a grove of palm trees and green lawns indicated that they had arrived at the Marrakesh station. The man jumped nimbly from the train and hurried off.

"He kept his face well concealed, did he not?" Christine said.

"It could have been that taxi driver," William surmised.

As the boys piled up their baggage on one side of the platform, Christine hailed two taxis. They were very small, and the young people had trouble squeezing into the narrow seats.

"We will drive to your hotel first," Christine said. "I picked the Manzur because it is quite close to our home."

As they neared the city, the wall that surrounded the ancient settlement loomed larger and larger. Located quite some distance apart were arched gates leading inside.

"Our home is built right against the other side of the wall," Christine explained as they approached one of the entrances.

Just then Chet spied an Arab standing beside a camel, waving to tourists and pointing to the animal.

"He's selling rides!" Chet said. "I want to sit on the camel!"

Christine asked their driver to stop, and the other cab pulled up in back.

"Go ahead," she said. "Try it."

The boys jumped out, smiling broadly, and

paid the Arab. The beast lowered itself on his command, and Chet stepped aboard. With a great lurch, the animal's back legs levered his rear into the air. Then the front legs unhinged as the camel stood up.

The man led it around in a circle.

"Whoopee!" Chet cried out.

Then the others took turns riding the camel. Joe was the last in line. As he climbed onto the camel's back, William drew Christine aside.

"See that man against the wall? Is he the one from the train?"

"I think so. Look at what he is doing!"

The man had pulled a camera from his djellabah and was snapping a picture of Joe!

"Maybe he took shots of all of you," Christine said. She looked worried.

William approached the man, but when the fellow saw him coming, he rose, turned, and disappeared in the crowd pushing through the gate.

William returned to the others and told them about the incident.

"What do you make of it, Frank?" he asked.

"I think it's bad news," Frank replied. "No doubt he took those pictures for a reason."

The boys and Christine piled into the taxis again and went on to the Manzur Hotel. It was old-fashioned and roomy, and the mosaic tiles under their feet resounded as they walked to the concierge's desk.

Christine waited until they had put their bags into their large room, the French window of which looked out over a lovely garden. Then she said, "Now come and meet my family. It is only a short walk."

The Cellier home was located at the far end of the hotel's extensive gardens. It was built of cement and red clay. On one side a stone stairway led to the top of the ramparts. "The view is beautiful from up there, especially at night," Christine said.

Inside, the travelers found a modern home with European decor, tastefully furnished. Dr. and Mrs. Cellier stood in the living room to meet them. Frank raised his eyebrows in surprise. No wonder, he thought, that Christine had such an odd and beautiful look. The doctor was an Oriental and his wife was a Frenchwoman.

After introductions had been made, Dr. Cellier chuckled. "Did Fenton tell you I was Vietnamese?"

"No," Joe said.

"Ah. Is that why you looked so surprised when you came in?" Cellier added with a wide grin.

The boys liked Christine's parents immediately. Mrs. Cellier was a charming woman with blond hair pulled back tightly.

"Have a seat and relax," she said in an accent that was much stronger than her daughter's. Conversation bounced back and forth as the Hardys told the Celliers about their father's work and their life in Bayport. Then Frank launched into a recital of the two cases that seemed to converge in Morocco.

The Celliers showed a great deal of interest in the mask and the secret map. "My husband knows a lot about Sijilmasa," Mrs. Cellier said.

"Yes," the doctor agreed. "I have been a student of North African history for years. The old city is buried, you know. Some day I would like to find it."

"Maybe we can search for it together," Chet said enthusiastically.

"Perhaps. I have been planning a holiday. We could rent jeeps and go on an expedition."

After an hour of animated conversation, the boys said good-by.

"I have a music lesson late this afternoon, but I will take you sightseeing tomorrow morning," Christine said. "How would you like to start with our *souq?*"

"That'll be great," Frank said as they left.

The boys spent the rest of the day swimming and diving in the hotel's pool, and lounging under palm trees in the garden. The heat had been blistering. But in the evening, a breeze flowed out of the desert and a refreshing coolness settled upon the town.

"It is like something out of the Arabian nights, is it not?" William said as they finished dinner.

"Sure is," Chet said. "All these exotic things, people, foods——" He yawned contentedly.

Christine arrived the next morning during breakfast and chatted with them until they had finished. "Now remember what you have to say most in the *souq*," she said.

"Oo-la-la," Chet said.

The girl laughed. "And do you know '*balik*'? It means attention—get out of the way."

"We've learned that," Joe said.

The quintet went off on foot, deeply inhaling the fresh morning air as they traversed the circular driveway leading onto the street. Half a mile farther on they came to another inner gate, beside which loomed the minaret of a mosque.

Passing through the gate, the boys were surprised to see a huge area comprising many acres. Part of it was a flat, open expanse, filled with a milling crowd, mostly in Arabic dress. On the left was a long, low, one-story enclosure.

"What's that?" asked Joe.

"The *souq*," Christine said. "Hundreds of stores open onto a lot of tiny lanes. They are all covered by slats of wood. And look over there!" She pointed to a circle of people gathered around a group of performers. "Story tellers and snake charmers. Arabs like to be entertained. See those jugglers from Nigeria? They have a *ju-ju* man with them today!"

The boys looked at each other in amazement but said nothing as Christine continued. "We will go into the *souq* first. Later we can watch the acrobats."

Once inside, the Hardys understood the reason for the slatted covering. The midday sun beating down on the market would have been unbearable without some protection. Now the rays shone in tesselated patterns on the dirt floor.

The aisles teemed with people. Customers wandered from stall to stall. Donkeys bearing produce pushed through the milling humanity. Shopkeepers, standing in front of their places, extolled their wares with rapid speech and gestures.

"This seems like a madhouse," Frank said as he walked in the lead with Christine.

"To us it is quite orderly," she said.

"Hey, Chet. Here's a sword place." Joe pointed to a stall next to a rug bazaar.

The boys stepped into the low, narrow store. Its walls were hung with scimitars, swords, bejeweled daggers, and radiant hunting knives.

The Americans, fascinated, examined the wares eagerly. The shopkeeper spoke French, and with Christine as an interpreter, they learned much about the exotic blades.

Seemingly from nowhere, another salesman appeared. More loquacious than the first, he had the advantage of knowing some English. He took

Frank by the arm and led him deeper and deeper into the store.

"The best things are in back!" he said.

Frank felt uneasy. When they reached the rear, the man pushed him through a doorway heavily hung with a curtain of beads.

Before the boy could protest, he found himself facing an Arab holding a magnificent dagger. The fellow grinned and approached the boy!

CHAPTER XVI

Ghost in the Souq

INSTANTLY Frank assumed a judo defense posture. If the man were to lunge, he would be ready! The thought of calling out flashed through his mind, but if the Arab were an assassin, he could strike before help arrived.

The boy emitted a low guttural challenge and watched for the slightest move from his adversary. But instead of the anticipated thrust, the man smiled benignly.

"You are not in danger," he said. "This part of the shop is a special place. It contains nothing but my very best merchandise."

He proffered the dagger and Frank took it in his hand. The blade, curved slightly, was finely honed and the haft was inlaid with beautiful copper work. Then the salesman showed him the sheath. It was made of leather and copper, intricately patterned in a red-and-blue design.

"This you will find nowhere else," the shop-keeper said. "But for you a special price."

When he quoted it, Frank remembered Christine's advice. *"La!"* he said. "Too much."

"Ah, you speak Arabic," the man said, nodding his head in appreciation. "You know something about our country. We will reduce the price. Only for you."

But the twenty percent reduction, Frank reasoned, was not enough. They haggled back and forth, and every time Frank turned to walk away, the man clutched his arm and lowered the price by a few more dollars.

Finally Frank made a counter-offer of half the original price. The shopkeeper rolled his eyes up, said his children would starve if he carried on business this way, and ended by saying, "Good. We have a bargain."

To make sure, Frank walked back into the main part of the shop to consult Christine. She agreed that the dagger was worth that much, and that it was a good buy.

Frank paid and showed his purchase to the others. "I'm going to hang it on the wall of our room as a memento of Marrakesh," he said.

As they stepped out of the shop, Joe asked Christine where the leather store was located. She said it was not far ahead. They continued pushing through the crowd, and as the sun rose higher, the colors of the interior became even more vivid. Displayed in front of a boutique was a sky-blue djellabah with a black face veil, also a shocking pink one with a purple veil.

William remarked that the clothes concealed the wearer's figures, so their identity was unknown.

"And what about the face?" Chet said. "All you can go by are the eyes. And every girl seems to have big brown eyes."

Joe laughed. "You came here to do a bit of detective work. Remember? Don't worry about the girls."

They stopped at another shop and watched a group of men sewing the embroidered caftans worn by women and adding gold braids and trimmings of colored sequins.

"Hey," Joe said, "if we get one for Mother, do you think she'd wear it?"

Frank laughed. "To a costume party maybe."

Farther on was a stand devoted to sandalwood from Indonesia. "This is burned for incense," Christine remarked and added, "Look, there is the leather-goods shop."

The stall was hung with all kinds of clothing made of leather. "It smells like a new football," Chet remarked, as he sniffed the air.

The owner spoke rapidly in French. Frank said, "Do you speak English?"

"Non, Monsieur." He looked sadly at them until Christine smiled and addressed him in the melodious language he was accustomed to.

Acting as their interpreter, she described a beautiful leather coat the boys had seen in the United States. It had carried a Paris label. Who could have bought it?

The man at first did not seem to understand, but suddenly his face brightened. "Yes," he said, "I made a few special garments for the French company and inserted the labels myself. But before I could ship them abroad, a customer bought one right here."

"Do you remember who he was?" Christine asked.

The leather man seemed pleased that praise for his work had reached America. *"Oui, Mademoiselle."*

He was about to open his mouth again, when his eyes fell on something in the crowd. A look of fright crossed his face. His mouth shut tight, and with a grim look he turned and walked to the rear of his shop.

"What'd he see?" Chet asked. "A ghost?"

"Maybe someone gave him the high sign to quit talking," was Frank's guess.

Christine added, "Perhaps it was the buyer himself!"

"We're being spied on," Joe declared. "There's no doubt about that!"

"Let's get out of here," Frank said.

"Hey, wait a minute," Chet said. "I've got my eye on that vest over there. Wouldn't that look great with my checkered sport jacket?"

Christine smiled and said, "I will stay with Chet and help him bargain."

"Okay, we'll meet you outside," Frank said, and the boys hurried off. They walked back through the teeming alley of the *souq*, glancing at everyone who wore European clothing. But Scott was not among them.

"And to think he may be living right here in Marrakesh," William said, frustrated.

"Not only that," Frank added. "He knows we're here."

"Probably has our photos, too," Joe put in. "Frank, this could be dangerous."

When they emerged from the *souq* into the glaring sunshine, the first thing they saw was the snake charmer.

"Let's watch the act," Frank suggested, "while Chet's making up his mind about that vest. No use to look for our elusive friend any more."

The snake charmer, bareheaded and dressed in a dirty djellabah, sat cross-legged before an earthen jar. About his shoulders was coiled a large black snake. He picked up a flute and began to play a weird, random tune.

A cobra's head appeared from the jar. Its eyes shone like black diamonds, and its tongue flickered as the hood rose ominously. Then, to the delight of the onlookers, the cobra swayed to and fro to the rhythm of the music.

The crowd, which had been sitting back some

fifteen feet or so, pressed in closer to watch the dancing snake. Most were Arabs, but a handful of gaping tourists were among them.

The music stopped. The snake charmer spoke harshly to the cobra and its head disappeared into the jar. Then he stood up with the large black snake still over his shoulders. He smiled, showing a gleaming gold tooth, and begged for coins.

The spectators flung a few in his direction, as did the Hardys and William. The man walked up to the trio, pulled the snake from over his head and offered to drape it on one of them.

William spoke a few words of Swahili, whereupon the man grinned broadly and nodded.

"I will try it," William said. "He says it is harmless."

With that the snake charmer put the reptile over the Jamaican boy's head, and William began to stroke it.

"This baby is really cold," he said.

The snake charmer now hissed a few words to his beast. Instantly the snake coiled around William's chest; then it covered his face, so the boy's shouts of protest became muffled grunts.

The man danced around, as Frank and Joe tried to pull the reptile from William's body. But it was like a band of steel!

"He'll be killed!" Joe stormed at the Arab. "Get it off!"

CHAPTER XVII

The Purple Vat

WHILE William and the Hardys struggled with the snake, the Arabs in the crowd laughed gleefully. Finally one of them, with a neat beard and spotless djellabah, touched Frank on the arm. He spoke good English.

"This is part of the act," he said. "The snake will not hurt your friend. You must pay the owner a fee, however, to get it off."

Frank whirled about. "How much?"

"You have United States dollars?"

"Yes."

"I suggest you give him one."

Frank whipped open his wallet and threw a greenback in the direction of the snake charmer. The man stepped forward to retrieve the money. Then he clapped the reptile on the head, spoke rapidly, and the snake let go. With a sinuous movement, it climbed back on its master's shoulders.

"Are you all right?" Joe asked William.

"It did not hurt me, but I was quite startled," the boy replied.

They looked about for Chet and Christine, who had not yet appeared. Joe grew impatient. "I'm going back into the shop," he said. "Meet you here in a little while."

He sidled through the murmuring crowd. Finally he saw his friends coming. Chet held a package under his arm.

"Where've you been?" Joe asked.

"We had to do quite a bit of bargaining after the shopkeeper decided to talk to us again," Christine explained.

"He had just what I wanted," Chet added, affectionately patting his package.

"Well, come on now," Joe said, "the fellows are waiting." He was about to tell them about the snake, when he happened to glance back toward the leather shop. He noticed a man in native dress duck into the place. A ray of sunlight flashed across his face for a split second.

"It's Scott! I'm sure it's Scott!" Joe exclaimed.

"What? Where?" Chet asked.

"He went into the shop. Look, you go and get the others. Christine and I will try to eavesdrop."

"But——" Chet began to protest.

"Vamoose!" Joe ordered, and gave him a push. Chet realized that this was no time to argue and left.

Joe and Christine pushed through toward the merchant's stall and stopped at the rug bazaar next to it.

"In here!" the boy whispered.

They wriggled into the hanging folds of a Persian rug, unnoticed by the proprietor, whose back was turned. Once concealed, they listened intently. Voices were coming from the leather shop. The men were speaking French. The man Joe thought was Scott, was being addressed as *Monsieur* Dubonnet. His new coat, the shopkeeper said, was not ready yet.

Christine translated in a hushed whisper.

"There has to be fine needlework in the lining," the artisan declared. "Give me a few more days, *Monsieur* Dubonnet."

"But I am very busy," was the annoyed reply. "I need it right away."

"I will send it to your home," the merchant offered.

"Good."

With his heart pounding, Joe heard the man give his address in French. "Did you get it, Christine?"

She bobbed her head.

Joe peeked out of the rug in time to see the man press money into the hand of the artisan.

"If you see or hear anything of those Americans again," he said, "let me know." Then he left.

The young people stepped out of hiding and Joe declared, "It's Scott for sure. Let's go after him!"

The man had concealed his face in the hood of the djellabah and was striding toward the exit of the *souq.*

"Here come the others now," Christine said.

Frank, Chet, and William passed Scott, nearly touching elbows. Joe gestured wildly, but Frank did not get the message. Instead he called out, "Joe, was that really Scott?"

"Yes!" Joe replied, pressing forward as fast as he could. "He just passed you. Come on, we can still chase him."

But the shouting had alerted the man. He dashed in and out among the shoppers, with the pursuers on his heels. The djellabah retarded Scott's speed somewhat, but nevertheless he kept a safe distance ahead as he crossed over the open area and dashed to a gate in the city wall.

"Balik! Balik!" Chet cried, and the Arabs melted to one side. Outside the wall, they found themselves on a broad, dusty street. It was cluttered with carts, donkeys, and decrepit old automobiles, chugging along and laden with produce for the market.

"We'll catch him this time!" Joe cried out as he tried to keep pace with William's long strides.

Finally the fugitive reached a narrow slit cut into the ramparts. It contained a row of steps leading to the top of the wall. The man raced up, with the others in pursuit. William reached the top of the stairs first, in time to see Scott glide over several flat roofs and disappear.

"There he goes!" William said.

The others were at the spot in seconds and looked down over the edge to see a strange sight. In an area of several acres stood huge open vats half filled with dyes. They were yellow, red, and purple. A pungent smell rose from them.

"What crazy swimming pools," Chet quipped.

"This is where wool is dyed," Christine said. "Usually many men work here, but today is a holiday."

"Scott must be hiding among those vats!" Frank said. He put a hand on the edge of the wall and vaulted down. The others followed.

The ground around the vats was mucky from dye that had dripped over the edges, and the boys slipped and slid in their haste to search around the gooey vats.

Finally Frank shouted, "There he is!"

Scott jumped up from behind his cover and ran off as fast as he could, the hem of his djellabah splashed with a rainbow of colors.

Joe was the first to get anywhere near him. With a desperate lunge, the young detective clawed at the cloak and stopped the man short.

"There he goes!" William said.

Scott turned on him, cursing in French. With strength that Joe had not anticipated, Scott pinned his arms to his sides and lifted him up to the rim of a purple vat! Looking down into the fluid, the boy flailed about furiously. If he were thrown into the dye, it might be fatal!

CHAPTER XVIII

The Sixty-Forty Deal

Joe struggled desperately. Finally he succeeded. Scott lost his grip and the boy fell down, into the muck outside the vat.

Scott crouched for a moment before darting off again. By this time the others had reached Joe and helped him up. Both his arms were purple.

"Hurry!" Christine said. "We must get him cleaned off right away. If the dye has sufficient time to set, his arms might be stained for a year!"

Too messy to use a taxi, they boosted and pulled one another up to the rooftop again, hurried down the stone steps, and jogged along the road toward the Cellier home.

Christine's mother greeted them at the door with a baffled look. "What happened?" she exclaimed.

"Joe fell near a dye vat," the girl said. "We

need some strong soap, Mother. If you bring it out, I will use the garden hose."

Mrs. Cellier returned with laundry soap and a box of washing detergent. Joe scrubbed for ten minutes, while his brother played the hose over his arms.

"I guess that's about all that'll come off now," Frank remarked finally.

Joe looked at his arms. They were still rather dark. William broke into a white-toothed smile and said, "Joe, now we are brothers! Can you lend me a dollar?"

As the others laughed, Joe playfully reached for his wallet. Then a look of horror crossed his face. "It's gone! My wallet's gone! It must have dropped beside the vat!"

"I remember Scott bending down," Frank said. "I'll bet he picked it up!"

"I will go back and look," William offered.

"I'm coming with you," Chet said.

While the others cleaned their shoes, the two hurried off. Half an hour later they returned to say that a diligent search had failed to produce the missing wallet.

"That does it!" Joe said in disgust. "Now Scott has the map!"

"What a rotten break," Frank agreed. "Lucky I've got the other copy."

"Now what?" Chet asked.

"We're going to Scott's apartment to see if we

can get that map back!" Frank said. "What was the address, Christine?"

The girl wrote it on a piece of paper. "I would go with you if I could," she said. "But I have a meeting with a scholarship committee. You see, I intend to study medicine in Paris next fall."

"We can find our way," Frank said. "Besides, we'd better not all go anyway. That would be too obvious."

It was decided that he and William would take on the assignment. They were to meet Joe and Chet later at the hotel.

"But I would advise," Christine said, "that you wear djellabahs."

"Good idea," Frank agreed. "Where do we get them?"

"My father has several. They will fit you."

Clothed in the Arab costumes, Frank and William set off immediately to the Gueliz, the French quarter where Scott-Dubonnet lived. Using a taxi, they found the street and stopped at the number indicated.

It was a small modern apartment house. The names of the tenants were listed above the mailboxes in the foyer.

"Here it is," William said. "Dubonnet. Second floor, apartment B."

The companions ascended the narrow stairs quietly and moved along the hall about half-a-dozen paces until they faced 2B. Voices could be heard inside.

"I'm glad they're speaking English!" Frank whispered.

Tossing back the hoods of their djellabahs, the boys pressed close to the door to eavesdrop. Unmistakably, two of the voices belonged to Scott and Sam Brown! The words of several others were indistinct.

Brown said, "Come in on the deal with us. When we capture the Hardys tonight, we'll force the secret of the mask from them."

Scott laughed as if enjoying a big joke.

"What's so funny about that?" Brown demanded, obviously annoyed.

"I have your secret already," was the reply.

Now Frank and William heard the crinkle of unfolding tissue. "Here it is," Scott said.

There was a moment of silence, followed by murmurs of disbelief.

"How did you get it?" This was Tiffany Stribling.

"How? Well, it took some doing, but that's my secret."

"Wait a minute," Brown said. "Here's the mask. Let's check this out."

Again silence, and the boys realized that the criminals must be confused by the upside-down reading of the lines traced on the tissue. After a few minutes, Stribling discovered what Chet had stumbled upon. "Pretty clever. It's reversed. This seems to be authentic."

Scott spoke again. "Now listen. We have money to finance this treasure hunt, and the map. We'll make a sixty-forty split. Sixty for us."

"Oh, no, you don't!" Brown said, his voice rising.

"Have it your way, then. We'll part company."

Mumbling and grumbling followed, after which Stribling said, "Aker took care of that gumshoe Hardy. What more do you want?"

"I want sixty-forty!" Scott replied harshly. "How do I know that your man really rubbed out the detective?"

"He did. George has never failed an assignment."

Frank turned ashen. Had his father paid with his life to pursue this case?

William whispered, "I am sorry, man. I am really sorry."

"All right, you win." Stribling said finally.

"Good," Scott said. "Here's money to get a couple of jeeps and supplies. We'll leave——"

Just then footsteps sounded at the bottom of the stairs.

"Let's go," Frank said quietly, pulling up his hood. The two boys started down the stairway. Frank stole a look at the man who pushed past them.

The cab driver from Casablanca!

"Pardon," he said and looked directly at the young detective. Then he cried out in alarm. "Dubonnet! Hurry!"

As the boys reached the foot of the stairs and raced out the door, they could hear a commotion behind them.

"There they go! Frank Hardy and an Arab!"

The boys found an alley and dashed through to a parallel street. A taxi passed by and they leaped into it. As it started off, their enemies, waving their arms and shouting, tried in vain to pursue them.

When the boys arrived at the hotel, they met Joe and Chet in the lobby.

"Did you get my wallet?" Joe asked. Then he noticed his brother's disturbed expression. "What's the matter? Did anything happen?"

"It's Dad," Frank replied, hardly able to control his voice. "They got him!"

"What?"

"Hold it. Now wait," William objected, trying to calm the grief-stricken boy. "Remember, Stribling said that Aker was *supposed* to get your father. But there is no proof! Even Tiffany does not know if his man was successful."

With tears welling in his eyes, Joe hastened to a telephone booth. "I'm phoning home."

It took twenty minutes for the call to go through, giving the boys anxious moments to consider their predicament.

"If anything has happened to Dad," Frank said, "we'll have to return to the States right away."

"Of course," William said. "But do not give up yet!"

Mrs. Hardy finally answered and was surprised to hear from the boys.

"How's Dad? Is he all right?" Joe blurted.

"Oh, I suppose so. But he isn't here right now."

"Where is he?"

"I really don't know. He took an overnight bag with him and said he'd get in touch with me later."

Joe bit his lip. What should he say?

"Is there anything wrong?" Mrs. Hardy asked.

"Well—maybe. But we don't know for sure. Mother, if you hear from Dad, will you have him get in touch with us at the Manzur Hotel or at the Celliers' in Marrakesh?"

"Yes. I'll tell him to call right away."

The boy looked bewildered as he hung up the phone.

"Good grief!" Chet said. "What are we going to do now?"

William spoke up. "Get the police and raid Dubonnet's apartment!"

The Jamaican's determined voice roused the Hardys, and they immediately agreed to the strategy. Since the boys were acquaintances of Dr. Cellier's, the police were cooperative. They accompanied the Americans to Dubonnet's place, but found it empty!

"It looks as if somebody left in a hurry," one of the officers said.

"Let's go back to the Celliers'," Joe decided. "If we want to continue with the treasure hunt, we'll have to act fast."

Christine was home, and when she and her parents heard about the afternoon's events, they were flabbergasted.

"I think your father would want you to pursue the case to the end," Dr. Cellier said. "And you had better stay here for the night. Then, in the morning, rent jeeps and some gear, like sleeping bags, and get detailed maps of the area around the lost city."

"Will you come with us?" Chet asked hopefully.

"I cannot go right now. But I will try to follow later."

After the boys had picked up their luggage at the hotel, Christine showed them into the guest room. It had a large French window looking out onto the ramparts of Marrakesh. Mrs. Cellier brought in a cot, and Christine got her sleeping bag. "We do not have enough room, really," Mrs. Cellier apologized. "But it is only for one night."

"Please don't worry about that," Frank said. "The accommodations are just fine."

The boys waited hopefully for a call from Bayport, but none came. Finally they went to sleep.

How long they had dozed off Joe did not know. But he was awakened by a noise. He sat bolt upright and adjusted his eyes to the moonlight streaming into the French window.

Now the others responded to his sudden movement. They looked, mouths agape, at a figure standing in the window. It was a man with his body painted in bright colors. He wore a grass skirt, but the most startling thing was his face. It was hideous. Obviously he was wearing a mask.

He spoke a few words, then leaped from the casement onto the top of the wall and disappeared.

"A *ju-ju* man!" William said, his throat dry.

"What did he say? Did you understand it?" Chet asked.

"Yes. He put a curse of death upon us!"

CHAPTER XIX

Figue Barbari

THE boys jumped out of bed and climbed through the window. When they reached the ramparts, however, the *ju-ju* man was out of sight, and they returned to their room.

"You don't believe in this curse stuff, do you, William?" asked Chet, trying to act unconcerned.

"N-no," the Jamaican replied. "Not entirely."

"Tell you what, William," Frank said. "Now that we have the whammy on us, you take this charm to ward off the wizard's power." He removed the lion's tooth from his neck and placed the chain over his friend's head.

"I'll try," William said.

The next morning they were up very early. They gave Dr. Cellier a duplicate of the map in case he could join them later, and said good-by to their hosts. Christine accompanied them to the business district, where Chet and William rented two jeeps, while tents, camping equipment, shovels, crowbars, and assorted digging tools were rounded up by the Hardys.

All the while one nagging question persisted. Would they or their enemies be first to find what lay at the end of the route of the mysterious caravan? Time was now more important than ever.

With their chores swiftly completed, the young detectives consulted a reliable road map Dr. Cellier had given them.

"Good-by, Christine," Joe said.

The girl shook hands with each one. "You will see a lot of little fortified villages along the way," she said. "These are called casbahs. The natives are usually very nice people. They are Berbers."

"Not Arabs, you mean?"

"No. The Berbers are blue-eyed Caucasians. Where they came from originally nobody seems to know. They live in the Atlas Mountains and are farmers or herders."

Frank drove one jeep and Joe the other, and they set off along the highway, which wound higher and higher through the mountains to the east.

For the first twenty miles the road was good, although seemingly little used. They passed very few cars along the way. Frank floored the accelerator for a while but had to ease off because the road narrowed and grew steeper.

"I wish this buggy had more zip," he said to William, who was seated beside him.

Several miles farther on they left the paved highway and jounced along hard-packed dirt and gravel. Just past a bend, William spied a goat in the middle of the road.

"Frank, look out!" he shouted.

Frank swerved and stood on the brake. The jeep missed the animal, but slewed around. The rear wheel dangled dangerously over a sharp culvert beside a foaming mountain stream.

The boys gingerly stepped out so as not to upset the jeep's balance. Joe pulled up beside them. It was not until then that they noticed five men standing below at the edge of the stream. They had built a small lagoon of stones, and inside the quiet water hundreds of potatoes bobbed around.

"How do you like that?" Chet exclaimed. "They're washing spuds!"

"Probably Berber farmers," said Frank as the men scrambled up the side of the gully and stood grinning at the foreigners.

One, a stubble-bearded fellow with a skull cap pointed to the car, then to the road, and nodded.

"You want to help?" William said. "Fine, lend us a hand."

The natives joined in to lift the jeep safely onto the road. When it was done, Chet noticed a bush laden with ripe figs at the side of the road. He picked a few, pointing first to the figs, then to his open mouth.

"Leave it to Chet to find something to eat," Joe said, laughing.

The Berber farmers looked at the boy and nodded.

Chet stuffed a fig into his mouth. Now one of the men frowned, shook his head, and indicated no.

"Why can't they make up their minds?" Chet asked while he chewed on the fruit. "This doesn't taste bad!"

Shortly after midday, as the road grew even rougher, Frank stopped briefly. No sign of the criminals.

"We're at a pretty high altitude now," Joe said. "Look at those clouds. They'll be down on top of us before we know it!"

An hour later, Joe's guess proved to be correct. A dense fog settled over the road, which threaded around the mountain passes perilously close to precipitous cliffs. Their speed was reduced to a crawl.

Finally Frank stopped and jumped out of his jeep to consult with Joe and Chet. William joined them.

"We'd better wait till the fog lifts," was Frank's advice. "I can't see more than a few feet. If we go over the edge, it'll be the end."

They waited for several hours. No traffic came from either direction.

"I am wondering," William said, "whether the Scott-Stribling gang is up ahead or trailing us."

"Either way," Frank said, "there's no use in worrying. This fog may have stopped them, too."

"I wish I could quit thinking about Dad," Joe said, "where he is, and what he's doing."

"He's always been able to take care of himself," Frank remarked. "You know, William, you may be right. Stribling could have been bluffing."

Now it grew dark, and as the boys were about to break out some sandwiches they had brought along, Chet said, "Wow! Have I got a stomach-ache!"

It rapidly grew worse, and the stout boy bent over with pain. "The figs! They were poisonous!" he cried.

"Holy crow!" Frank muttered. "I hope not!" He was just about to reach for their first-aid kit to find the Alka-Seltzer, when William put a hand on his shoulder.

"Look!" he said.

Several figures appeared across the road. They moved slowly, their djellabahs blending into the heavy fog like wandering spirits.

As Chet began to moan, they came closer to

look at him. Then a man said in hesitating English, "Are you in trouble?"

"We sure are," Frank replied. "Chet must have been poisoned by figs."

"Figue barbari?"

"They were growing by the side of the road."

"Not poisonous," the man replied. "But they must be cooked." He told them that he had worked in Tangier for a year and that he and the others lived in a little settlement nearby.

"You come with us," he concluded.

The Berbers led the boys into a village consisting of a few huts made of rock and mud. Chickens darted around and the noise of goats could be heard through the fog. Dogs barked as they drew closer.

They were taken into one of the huts, where a family of friendly blue-eyed people smiled and nodded while the boys described their travels to the interpreter. Then they were served bread and goat meat and were led into a small anteroom. Its walls were lined with crude bunks.

Chet, meanwhile, having learned that he was not about to die, improved quickly, and by the time they all lay down on the straw bedding, he felt much better.

Neither Frank nor Joe slept well during the night. The noise of chickens and the occasional barking of dogs sounded eerily through the thick fog, which continued to blanket the mountaintop.

By morning it had lifted, however, and when the Hardys opened their eyes, Chet was already up. He peered out of a window and let out a gurgling scream!

"Help! I'm nuts!" he wailed. "I've gone cuckoo!"

William was first to rush to his side and look out. There, in a scrubby tree in front of the hut, a goat was climbing in the topmost branches!

William laughed. "Chet, you are not daft. I have heard about these goats. They really do climb trees!"

"Phew!" Chet said. "I thought I was hallucinating from the *figue barbari*."

The farmer and his wife were preparing breakfast, but Frank said, "We have food in the car and will bring it in." With gestures he indicated what he meant, then hurried to the jeep with William. They were digging under a tarpaulin for their supplies when a sudden rumbling sound filled the air. Chet and Joe ran out to see what the noise was and froze in fright!

Rocks, boulders, and debris crashed down the side of the mountain with the roar of a hundred jets! The two jeeps were directly in the path!

"A rockslide!" Joe cried. "Frank, William, run!"

CHAPTER XX

The Mysterious Mirage

FRANK and William looked up in time to see what was happening. Racing for their lives, they were pelted with small stones that stung their backs and arms.

Then a huge boulder crashed like a thunderclap into the provisions jeep, sending it far over the edge of the cliff and into the valley below.

The boys reached the hut, where Joe and Chet were viewing the spectacle with terror. They watched as the second jeep was showered with dirt and pebbles.

Then it was all over. Quiet settled over the mountain once again. The little settlement had been spared, but not by much. Cautiously, the Berbers came out of their huts, talking excitedly.

"Wow!" Frank said, his hands still shaking. "That was close."

William nodded. "We were fortunate, but we lost a jeep."

The Berbers helped free the remaining one, which was laden with spare gasoline and digging tools.

"We'll have to carry on with only one vehicle," Frank said, rubbing his sore shoulders.

"I wonder if the *ju-ju* man's curse is working," William said. He fingered the lion's tooth charm. "Baby, do your thing! Wipe out the curse!"

The Berbers supplied the boys with bread, goat cheese, and water, and waved them off on their journey. Joe and Chet sat high on their equipment, with Frank at the wheel and William beside him. The road became even narrower, winding like a serpent coiled on the rim of the mountain.

William's finger followed their progress on the map spread out on his lap. "We are getting close to Rissani," he said. "The buried ruins of Sijilmasa should be around here somewhere."

With their destination near, a new exhilaration gripped the adventurers. Joe put the binoculars to his eyes and studied the deep valley below. "That must be Rissani," he said.

The road that had tilted up so many miles now descended rapidly and before long they were driving past the Rissani casbah.

"From here it's compass work," Frank said as

Frank and William raced for their lives!

he pulled to a stop outside the town. He took the death-mask-tissue map from his wallet, and with William he studied the lines. From Rissani the trail went south and west in a looping arc.

Frank was in favor of stopping at Rissani to ask a few questions, but was out-voted by the others.

"We need every minute of time," Joe argued.

"But we might pick up a clue," Frank reasoned. "Maybe the gang stopped here for something or other."

"So what if they did?" Chet said. "Let's not waste any time, Frank."

William agreed, and they kept on.

"What's over there?" Chet said, shading his eyes. "Another mountain?"

"It's a cliff," Joe announced. "Here, have a look."

The binoculars were passed around, and each of them surveyed the barrier that lay about thirty miles distant.

Joe spelled Frank at the wheel and William climbed up on the back with Chet. Now they realized that the desert, which had seemed to be so flat, was studded with outcrops of rocks between which steep dunes rippled like waves on a beach.

Coming to the top of a small rise, Frank studied the cliff again. "We don't seem to be any closer to it," he said. "Look!"

"What's the matter?" Chet asked.

"Camels!"

"You're seeing things. Nothing's there," Joe said.

"I guess you're right. Now I don't see anything —wait a minute! They are camels all right!"

Each of the boys scanned the shimmering expanse in front of them. The heat waves danced off the sand, obscuring and then revealing what appeared to be a small caravan. Suddenly, everything disappeared.

"It is a mirage," William said. "Deserts are known for them."

"Maybe it's the mysterious caravan written about on the death mask!" Chet said.

The boys stopped now and then to sweep the desert with their binoculars. Once Chet reported sighting seven camels, but Joe gently suggested that it was his imagination. There was no sign of jeeps and they were confident that their enemies were far behind them.

"The sun is apt to get you out here," Joe said.

Nonetheless, Frank ordered a sharp lookout for camel tracks. But he had to admit after another ten miles of driving, that the wind might have blown sand over any vestige of animal footprints.

Gradually the cliff loomed larger, and a cleft was clearly visible. It ran diagonally from the sand up into the top.

"I suppose we have to move south around this obstacle," Chet said.

"Not till we reach the base," Frank remarked.

"Could this be the end of the journey taken by the mysterious caravan?" William asked.

"It's possible," Joe said, and the boys wondered about it as they drove even closer to the escarpment. Now it stood only a few miles away, and the cleft in the rocks had grown to fantastic proportions.

"There may be a road running right through the cliff," William said.

"We'll have to explore it, Frank," Joe urged.

"Right. But in case anybody's there, I'll scout it first." He worked his way inside and returned shortly with word that he had not seen a sign of anybody.

The Hardys scanned the desert again to make sure they were not being followed. But nothing moved on the stark landscape.

Now they drove in, stopped, and appraised their situation. "No road," Frank noted. A quarter mile ahead of them the defile narrowed and the gray rocks towered so high they had to crane their necks to see the top.

"We'd better turn around and get out of here," Chet said.

Frank nodded and started back. Another, smaller, cleft became visible.

"I wonder what's in there," Joe said. "Think we should find out?"

"What if it's a cave without bottom?" Chet said. "We might fall all the way down."

"And land in China?" Joe quipped.

"All right, explore it if you want," Chet said.

Leaving their jeep, the boys decided to go in, but they stationed Joe outside in the desert as a guard.

"If you see anything, holler," Frank told him.

"Roger," Joe said.

Frank, Chet, and William pushed into the narrow cleft and suddenly found themselves at the mouth of a cave. Its entrance was partially sealed by crumbling stones.

"Look, somebody put these together with mud mortar," William observed. They pulled away at the loose rocks. Age-old dust rose into their faces and made them cough.

"It's pretty dark in here," Frank said. "We need a flashlight."

"I'll get it," Chet volunteered. He went back to the jeep and returned with one. Its six-inch lens sent a powerful beam to the back of the cave. Just then Joe came in.

"I saw an airplane going overhead in a direct line," he reported. "Do you think it could be our enemies spying on us?"

"Maybe. Better watch it," Frank advised.

Joe's eyes, slowly becoming accustomed to the dark, focused on the cavern floor.

"Holy crow, look at this!" he exclaimed." Skeletons!"

The bones of five men, laid out side by side, rested stark on the ground. The skulls grinned ludicrously at the boys, who stepped over them gingerly.

Farther back they came upon small piles of dust and pebbles, and the remnants of leather sacks that had crumbled with age. Frank bent down and rubbed the dust between his fingers.

"Gold!" he cried out. "Gold! We've found the treasure!"

"You have done us a great favor!" The harsh voice behind them sounded familiar. The boys whirled about. Several men, clothed in djellabahs, advanced toward them.

Their enemies!

The speaker was Scott. His face was now clearly visible. Beside him was the phony taxi driver and Jason Hickson, who had fled to Casablanca. Farther back were Stribling and Brown. The rest of the men were dark-faced strangers.

The boys realized that the camel caravan had been no mirage! The criminals had been ahead of them after all and must have hidden behind a dune, allowing the Hardys and their friends to complete the discovery!

Stribling spoke. "You were most kind, gentlemen, to lead us to the treasure. What fools you were to think you could outfox us."

"All right," Frank said, trying to keep his cool. "You win. Here's the treasure. It's all yours. Just let us out of here."

"Frank," Joe whispered, "we can't do that. Let's fight 'em!"

Dubonnet-Scott laughed loudly. "Of course the treasure is ours, and of course you're not going to fight us. You won't escape, either. We'll leave you right here with the other skeletons!" He kicked a pile of bones, and a tibia skittered across the cave.

As their enemies approached menacingly, Frank, Joe, and Chet held up their fists in self-defense. But William whispered, "Frank, those black men. They are the acrobats from Marrakesh. And the small one is the *ju-ju* man. I'm sure of it!" With that he whipped the African charm from around his neck. He stepped forward and spoke in Swahili.

The *ju-ju* man shrank back, as did the acrobats, and they murmured among themselves.

"What did you tell them?" Joe asked.

"I said I was a more powerful *ju-ju*. I would put a terrible curse on them unless they defeated their confederates."

Seconds later a fracas broke out, and the cave

reverberated with shouts, screams, and curses. The agile acrobats pounced on the criminals and even before the Americans could pitch in, their adversaries lay subdued, moaning, begging for mercy, and rubbing their bruises.

Suddenly a clear voice rang through the cavern. "Stand where you are, all of you!"

"It's Dad!" Joe cried out.

"Nobody move. We have you covered." It was the commanding voice of Fenton Hardy again. Joe raced forward and flung his arms around his father. "We thought you were dead!"

"A base canard!" the detective said with a grin. "An inexcusable exaggeration!"

Lined up behind him with weapons poised stood Dr. Cellier and two police officers.

Stribling looked up in disbelief. "But—but Aker was supposed to have rubbed you out!"

"He tried," Mr. Hardy said. "But I laid a trap for him. Then I caught two of your men. Mr. Dingo, Scott's chauffeur, confessed everything!"

Dingo had been left behind to see that Aker did his job properly, but both had fallen prey to the detective. "It was Dingo," Mr. Hardy said, as the police handcuffed everyone except the acrobats and the *ju-ju* man, "who led us to the World-Travel Agency in Casablanca. In the cellar under it we found thousands of blank tickets, name plates, sucker lists, and paraphernalia used in the racket all over the world."

"And when your Dad contacted me," Dr. Cellier added, "I told him where you had gone."

"Great!" Frank exclaimed. "But how did you find us here?"

"We hired a plane and spied Joe outside."

"What I would like to know," Frank said, "is how did you know we were going to Africa, Mr. Scott? You must have shadowed us all along."

"None of your business!" Scott grumbled.

But Brown, obviously hoping to make things easier for himself if he talked, gave the answer. "We did. When your fat friend picked up the tickets, we followed him. Then one of our men took the same plane."

"Shut up!" Scott growled.

"But how did you ever combine forces with Scott?" Frank pressed on.

Brown was silent, but Mr. Hardy reported that a spy from each group had been scouting the Hardy home and by accident had run into each other. Finding they had a common enemy, though two diverse causes, they melted into one gang.

"But why did Scott impersonate the Jamaican envoy and try to get the mask from us at the same time that the kidnapping exchange was being set up?" Frank asked.

"It would have been easier that way," Mr. Hardy said. "But since it didn't work, they went through with the exchange."

"And once we were in Casablanca, Scott tried to do away with us through that phony note from Klem!" Joe said accusingly.

Scott's face was expressionless.

"And when that didn't work, he set our hotel room afire!" Joe added.

Scott shrugged. "Prove it!"

"And you were the man sitting across the aisle from us in the train to Marrakesh!" William said. "The Frenchman in Arab disguise, who rolled his bread into little balls."

"How did they know we were going to Marrakesh?" Chet asked. "They lost our trail when we left the Marhaba!"

"We went back to the travel agency the next morning, remember?" Joe said. "No doubt that man on the roof was one of their gang, and he followed us."

The next question was where the crooks got the camels. It was revealed that Stribling, who knew the ways of the desert, had sent ahead for a caravan to wait in readiness at Rissani.

Frank said, "We might have discovered this had we stopped there and asked a few questions."

Joe's face grew red. "You win, Frank. Never leave a stone unturned."

A celebration was held the following night in the Cellier home. During the evening Frank whispered to Christine, "May I use your phone, please? I want to call home."

In the next room he talked quietly to his mother, and when he returned, Chet said, "What's up? You look happy as a clam at high tide."

"Ask me no questions and I'll tell you no lies."

Three days later, the missions of father and sons having been brought to a successful conclusion, the Hardys and their friends touched down at Bayport Airport. As they all trooped into the house at Elm Street, a surprise was waiting. Tony, Biff, and Phil greeted them with grins on their faces, and the women hugged them. In the middle of the living room stood a wire-mesh cage. In it a dog paced about, sniffing at the arrivals and making odd, chortling noises.

"It's for you, William," Mrs. Hardy said. She turned to Frank. "I did have quite a job finding a Basenji breeder, but I managed!"

William stood tongue-tied for a few moments. His eyes widened as he looked from face to face and then at the cage.

"Thank you. Oh, thank you so much," he finally said, opening the top. Out jumped the lithe animal, pointed ears alert, and pranced around the room. Then he sprang into William's open arms, nuzzled him, and licked his face.

"Okay, okay!" the boy laughed. "I am glad to see you, too!"

"He can tell a *ju-ju* man from just any ordinary fellow, see?" Joe quipped. "Smart dog!"

Even Aunt Gertrude smiled and nodded, while the happy reunion went on for another hour. It was fortunate that the Hardys could not foresee the future, because around the next bend lurked a treacherous and frightening mystery to be known as *The Witch Master's Key*.